CHARITY
ANGEL CREEK CHRISTMAS BRIDES
BOOK ONE

SYLVIA MCDANIEL

A Mail-Order Bride, Secrets, Lies, and a Christmas Miracle

Five Charleston women desperate for marriage-minded men and the chance to rebuild their lives after the Civil War answer an ad in the Groom's Gazette. Charity Kingston has to get out of Charleston or face life working in a brothel. But the past follows her to Angel Creek, Montana, revealing her Irish temper. And the bordello owner demands payment of her debt.

After leaving the military, Lewis Brown is given a chance at a new start in life. Taking a dead man's identity, he begins fresh as a saloon owner in Angel Creek. Imagine his surprise when a mail-order bride comes with the saloon. In a twist of fate, his past is exposed, his secrets revealed, and his worst nightmare confirmed.

Lewis and Charity need a Christmas Miracle.

Charleston isn't what it used to be. The war has left it in ruins and the chance of a suitable marriage almost obsolete. Five friends take a daring leap and head west for a new life and possible love match as Mail-Order brides. After finding their happily ever afters, they invite more of their friends to join them, and soon, Angel Creek, Montana is invaded by Southern Belles all looking for love and the town will never be the same.

CHRISTMAS 2018 BOOKS
Book 1: Charity — Sylvia McDaniel
Book 2: Julia — Lily Graison
Book 3: Ruby — Hildie McQueen
Book 4: Sarah — Peggy McKenzie
Book 5: Anna — Everly West

CHRISTMAS 2019 BOOKS
Book 6: Caroline — Lily Graison
Book 7: Melody — Caroline Clemmons
Book 8: Emma — Peggy McKenzie
Book 9: Viola — Cyndi Raye
Book 10: Ginger — Sylvia McDaniel

CHRISTMAS 2020 BOOKS
Book 11: Abigail — Peggy McKenzie
Book 12: Pearl — Hildie McQueen
Book 13: Rebecca — Lily Graison
Book 14: Charlotte — Kari Trumbo
Book 15: Minnie — Sylvia McDaniel
Book 16: Adele — Cynthia Woolf

Book 17: Victoria — Maxine Douglas
Book 18: Meg — Caroline Clemmons

CHRISTMAS 2021 BOOKS
Book 19: Glenda — Hildie McQueen
Book 20: Temperance — Lily Graison
Book 21: Hannah — Peggy McKenzie
Book 22: Amy — Caroline Clemmons
Book 23: Cora — Sylvia McDaniel

Find Them All At Amazon.Com

Look for the new series Mistletoe Falls Christmas Brides

CHAPTER 1

*C*hristmas Eve 1914

At nearly seventy years of age, Charity stepped into the living room where the children sat around the tree, anxiously awaiting the adults. Not as patiently as she had hoped as she watched Mick wrestle Christopher to the ground.

Glancing around, she felt so blessed as she stared at the little ones descended from her and her friends. Who would ever have thought five mail-order brides from Charleston would be so fortunate?

"Great-grandmother, tell us the story of how you came to Angel Creek."

"Child, you have heard that tale many a time," she said, pulling the girl to her, knowing any holiday spent with friends and family could be her last.

"Tell it again." Her nine-year-old great-granddaughter Sarah —named after her best friend—said, dancing.

Little Sarah slipped her hand into hers and led her to a rocker in the corner as everyone gathered around her.

Her heart swelled with so much love, tears sprang to her eyes.

She glanced up just as her friend, the older Sarah came into the room. "Charity, are you going to tell that story again?"

"The children want to hear it," she replied wanting one last remembrance of that trying time.

"Please," they cried in unison.

Julia one of the original brides, grinned and nodded. "It's a beautiful story."

"A Christmas story," Charity said smiling. "Of hope after such a terrible time."

"Of love and happiness," Ruby, another one of the brides said sticking her head in the door.

There was much Charity didn't tell the younger generation, because some things were meant for grown-ups, but always the trials and tribulations remained the same.

"Wait for me," Anna said, the last of the five brides, as she used her cane to walk to the nearest chair. Somehow they were all still alive, the oldest pushing eighty with the families they'd longed for.

"After the Civil War, very few young men returned to Charleston, South Carolina. Many men died during the war or never came home. Leaving five young lady friends, all wanting husbands and children, believing they would be old maids or worse."

The children laughed.

"Including me, until we became mail-order brides..."

Summer 1865

Standing in the sunlight, a cold wind blew Lewis Brown's hair into his eyes as he piled the last few rocks onto the grave and stood. Out of respect, he removed his hat. He felt the urge to say a few words as he stared at the mound of dirt for the man he'd just buried.

In the week they knew each other, they'd become brothers. Both with overbearing fathers who wanted to control their sons.

"Jakob, we didn't know one another very long, but I want to tell you thanks for giving me a second chance. You were a good man and we shared a lot in common. Two interfering fathers."

He pulled out the letter and read it once again. "I'll do my best to do your name proud and I'll always be grateful for your gift. Rest in peace, dear friend."

The snort of a nearby horse had Lewis glancing around nervously. One-Eyed Jack still searched for Jakob with the intent to finish him off, but that was no longer a problem. In the end, ol' Jack's bullet had done him in, but Jakob would live on.

In Angel Creek, Montana, Jakob's father purchased a saloon trying to get his wayward son to settle down. And now he would.

FALL 1865

Charity Kingston knew something had to change. After the Civil War ended, the redistribution of wealth and property was quick. Pay your assessed taxes or lose your home.

The letter informing her the house would be auctioned arrived months ago. The fees were enormous and she sold everything to pay the overdue taxes, but it wasn't enough. The riches she enjoyed, her father put into confederate money. Now that paper was worthless.

In fact, she used it to start the fireplace this winter. Along with whatever furniture she could burn. The only thing she learned during the Great War was men were irrational when it came to honor and dignity. And now thousands of young men had died for a cause that left them all poor and hungry and lonely.

So many of the young men of Charleston were killed on the battlefields, leaving an entire generation of young women with no one to consider marrying.

She picked up the Groom's Gazette, a newspaper she'd splurged on. *Women wanted. Angel Creek, Montana. Men seeking wives.* A chance to start over. It would mean abandoning everything she loved.

Could she leave this grand old house, her parents' graves and her friends?

A rapid knock on the door sounded and she sighed, wondering if this was the new owners come to take the house and put her out in the streets. For weeks, she'd expected to be forced from her home.

Sooner or later, she would face them. She walked to the door and slowly pulled it open.

"Miss Kingston?" a dapper looking man said, gazing at her.

The suit he wore was elegant on the handsome, pompous man. All he needed was a carpet bag in his hand and she would know he was not from this area.

"Yes," she said.

"John Roberts III," he said, holding out his hand. "I've come with a proposition for you. May I come in?"

When her mother and father had been alive, she was told to never allow a man entry into the home when she was alone. But times had changed. Everyone was gone, and in the last year, she'd taught herself a thing or two about protecting herself. A revolver worked wonders.

"What is it you want to talk about?"

"Your home. I'm going to purchase it," he said.

With a sigh, she knew this day would soon come, but that didn't make it any easier.

"Come in, Mr. Roberts. We can sit in the parlor," she said. "Somehow, I don't think this is a conversation I'm going to enjoy."

He gave her a smile that didn't quite reach his eyes and a shiver went through her at his cocky air. Leading the way into the only room with furniture, all the other pieces she sold or traded for food. She sank down in the chair, forcing him to sit on her mother's favorite sofa. The only one left in the house. The only one she hadn't been able to part with yet.

"When do you expect me out?"

"I have an opportunity for you. Do you recognize me?"

"Your face is a little familiar, but I can't remember where we met."

"Have you heard of the Charleston Gentleman's Club?" he asked. "In one month, I'll own your home and my plans are to turn it into a place where upper class gentleman will be entertained."

A sick queasiness filled her stomach as she remembered hearing rumors about the place. A bordello, which only accepted the most beautiful women. A place where carpetbaggers spent time with the ladies.

His eyes swept over her, lingering on her breasts. Nausea was quickly replaced with anger firing like a match striking flint. The nerve of this pompous ass to think she would become one of his women. No, no, no. No matter how desperate she became, she would not live her life as a whore, letting men have their way with her.

"As long as you work for me, I'm prepared to let you stay in this house. It will become a place where discerning gentleman spend time with you or any of the girls living here."

Her mother must've been turning over in her grave at this moment. The thought of her family home becoming a whorehouse was too much.

"Are you a virgin?"

The question had her Irish temper sparking, ready to erupt.

"That, sir, is none of your business."

A smile spread across his face. "So you are. Great. As beautiful as you are, your virginity will bring a high price. We'll hold an auction and split the proceeds. With all that gorgeous auburn hair, you'll fetch a nice sum of money."

The hell she would.

Glancing around the place, he shook his head. "The house will need a lot of work to get ready. You'll be able to remain here in your home as long as you are one of my girls."

Her hands clenched, her Irish ire surging like a gator chasing prey through the swampland. Taking a deep breath, she reminded herself it would be better to appear cordial than to outright denounce his scheme. Better to make arrangements to escape than unleash her volatile temper on the pimp.

Wanting him out of the house now, she stood. "Mr. Roberts, I think it's time you left."

"I'll give you time to contemplate my proposal. The tax office said we'll close in thirty days. After that, I'll be sending the workers over to do reconstruction. Once the home is ready, we'll open for business and hold the auction."

Rising, he smiled at her and then he reached out and ran his hand down her cheek. No man touched her and she reacted by slapping the man. "Get out of my house, now."

He grinned. "You've got spunk. Your beauty will make us both a lot of money. If you decide against my offer, be out of the house by the first of next month."

The man needed to leave now, before her temper exploded. She walked to the front door and opened it. While she still owned her home, she had control over the trash.

"Good day, Mr. Roberts."

With a tip of his hat, he strolled onto the sidewalk and she slammed the door. Time to meet with the girls and tell them of her decision—to leave. How wonderful it would be if they decided to join her in Montana.

CHAPTER 2

*T*ime was running out. Like every Monday, Charity marched up to the door of her friend Anna's home, only this time she had a mission. Sure, they all worked on wedding quilts, dreaming of their big day, but that seemed impossible now.

Last night, she spent time pouring over the Groom's Gazette, plotting her escape from John Roberts III.

Without knocking, she opened the door to find her friends sitting with their heads bowed over their needlework. The somber mood of the room was the exact opposite of how Charity felt at the moment. Bursting with exciting news to share, she could hardly contain herself.

"Good morning, ladies. Hard at work already."

"Good morning," Anna mumbled. "Yes, working on a quilt I never will use."

Julia tossed her needlework aside. "We're wasting our time."

The last few weeks, sadness had prevailed as they came to the conclusion few young men would return from the war. Those who made it home were quickly snatched up by more eligible younger women.

At twenty-one years of age, society considered them sitting on the shelf. Old maids. Spinsters. Prigs. Prudes. None of these words fit them, but they applied to the five friends.

Ruby started to cry. "We'll never have husbands and children."

Before the blubbering became a wail storm of tears, Charity had to tell them. "Stop crying. Wipe your eyes. I've found a solution."

The four women gazed at her, their eyes wide. Frowns wrinkled each forehead, skepticism shadowing their gazes.

"Well, don't keep us in suspense," Julia said.

Charity pulled out the newspaper she hid in her skirts.

"What is it?" Sarah asked.

"A Groom's Gazette. Men place ads in here for a wife. A small town in Montana, Angel Creek, is asking for five women. It's perfect for us."

They stared at her like she had lost her mind. "Angel Creek needs women. We need husbands. We'd all be together. This would give us an opportunity to have everything we want."

Most of all, she no longer would need to hide from Mr. Roberts. A shudder rippled through her at the thought of it.

The ladies all stared at her with a mixture of horror. Yet she could see they were considering the idea of traveling to a place where they could start over.

"We would be mail-order brides," Charity said.

Anna blurted out, "I'm willing to sign up to be a mail-order bride."

Ruby chimed in. "Me too."

Staring at Sarah, her best friend who needed to escape the city, Charity wanted so badly for her to come. "It would be a way to sneak Becca out of town."

"Yes, I'll do it," Sarah said.

In unison, all eyes turned to Julia. She was their "look twice before she leaped" member of their group. Soft spoken, yes, but her courage and determination were as strong--if not stronger than--everyone else's. So was her need for a fresh beginning.

Sarah cupped her hand over Julia's. "There's safety in numbers. No one will be alone. If one goes, we all go. Our friendship and support could be just like here."

A hush fell over the parlor and Charity held her breath, really, really hoping Julia would agree. A heartbeat later, Julia sighed and looked every one of them square in the eyes. "Oh, yes, I'll join, as long as we all go to the same place."

A nervous wave of snickering rippled over the women as they realized their decision. A chance at a real life not hampered by war.

Charity squared her shoulders and exclaimed, "Let's go!"

"All of us could be married before Christmas," Anna said.

"And possibly children by next fall," Ruby said with a smile.

The five girls stood and wrapped their arms around each other like they did whenever times grew tough and they needed reassurance from one another. Bowing their heads, they suddenly jumped up and down and squealed.

A new beginning. A new chance at life.

For Charity, an escape from Charleston's most famous bordello.

A MONTH later it was Charity's last night in her home. The only place she had ever lived. Yet, she knew she couldn't stay, which left her sad, but part of her also thought this was a new beginning. A new opportunity in life, which not only excited her, but made her nervous.

This afternoon, after visiting her parents' graves one last time, she came home to find a box waiting on the door step. Eagerly she opened it wondering if one of her distant relatives or friends had sent her a going away present, though she told very few people her plans.

Inside she discovered the most beautiful white dress. Lacy white with a clinging bodice that dipped dangerously low in the front and tight to her hips. Had her groom shipped her this beautiful gown as a surprise? Looking inside, she found the card.

For the auction. This dress will enhance your curves and make your beauty shine. We will both make a lot of money. John Roberts III

A rush of pure rage surged through her. The man assumed she would be *his* whore. That she would allow men to touch her body just so she could remain in her home. A home he would change and turn into a place where his naughty business could be conducted by his rich friends.

Oh, hell no, she would no longer accept being treated liked a second-class citizen. Enough.

Jumping up, she ran and found the scissors. Though it wasn't the dress's fault, she couldn't stop the anger that pumped through her veins leaving her shaking. She cut the fabric and then ripped the gown to shreds. When she was finished, the beautiful gown was in tatters unfit to be worn.

Still full of fury at the unfairness of life, she found her father's hammer and began to exact her fury on rooms where Mr. Roberts's girls would conduct their business. In a frenzy, she went into the bedrooms, destroying anything of value, creating gaping holes in the walls and a trail of damage.

Damn him for taking the last meaningful thing in her life. Damn him for trying to coerce her into staying and being a prostitute. And damn him for reeking of wealth and power and making her feel small. Well, no more.

Finally she tired and when she glanced down she saw plaster covered her dress. The floors were littered with her demolition. A sadness overcame her at the destruction she created and she sank to the floor and cried.

The home she loved would never be the same and neither would Charity. The war had taken everything from her, but after tonight, she would cry no more. Never again would she find herself penniless. Never again, would she be alone and homeless. Never again, would a man think he could make her his whore.

John Roberts III may have won the war, but she certainly left him a mess to clean up. Glancing at the carnage, a giggle erupted from her. The man was in for quite a shock. Amazing what her temper could devise.

Tomorrow would begin her new life. As much as she hated to leave Charleston, she would embrace her new situation and make the best of it. No more tears over everything she lost. At the end of this journey, a new beginning and a husband.

A month later it was Charity's last night in her home. The only place she had ever lived. Yet, she knew she couldn't stay, which left her sad, but part of her also thought this was a new beginning. A new opportunity in life, which not only excited her, but made her nervous.

This afternoon, after visiting her parents' graves one last time, she came home to find a box waiting on the door step. Eagerly she opened it wondering if one of her distant relatives or friends had sent her a going away present, though she told very few people her plans.

Inside she discovered the most beautiful white dress. Lacy white with a clinging bodice that dipped dangerously low in the front and tight to her hips. Had her groom shipped her this beautiful gown as a surprise? Looking inside, she found the card.

For the auction. This dress will enhance your curves and make your beauty shine. We will both make a lot of money. John Roberts III

A rush of pure rage surged through her. The man assumed she would be *his* whore. That she would allow men to touch her body just so she could remain in her home. A home he would change and turn into a place where his naughty business could be conducted by his rich friends.

Oh, hell no, she would no longer accept being treated liked a second-class citizen. Enough.

Jumping up, she ran and found the scissors. Though it wasn't the dress's fault, she couldn't stop the anger that pumped through her veins leaving her shaking. She cut the fabric and then ripped the gown to shreds. When she was finished, the beautiful gown was in tatters unfit to be worn.

Still full of fury at the unfairness of life, she found her father's hammer and began to exact her fury on rooms where Mr. Roberts's girls would conduct their business. In a frenzy, she went into the bedrooms, destroying anything of value, creating gaping holes in the walls and a trail of damage.

Damn him for taking the last meaningful thing in her life. Damn him for trying to coerce her into staying and being a prostitute. And damn him for reeking of wealth and power and making her feel small. Well, no more.

Finally she tired and when she glanced down she saw plaster covered her dress. The floors were littered with her demolition. A sadness overcame her at the destruction she created and she sank to the floor and cried.

The home she loved would never be the same and neither would Charity. The war had taken everything from her, but after tonight, she would cry no more. Never again would she find herself penniless. Never again, would she be alone and homeless. Never again, would a man think he could make her his whore.

John Roberts III may have won the war, but she certainly left him a mess to clean up. Glancing at the carnage, a giggle erupted from her. The man was in for quite a shock. Amazing what her temper could devise.

Tomorrow would begin her new life. As much as she hated to leave Charleston, she would embrace her new situation and make the best of it. No more tears over everything she lost. At the end of this journey, a new beginning and a husband.

AFTER WHAT SEEMED LIKE FOREVER, Charity couldn't believe they finally arrived in Angel Creek. The long journey was over and now they would soon face the men who paid for them to travel all that way from Charleston.

When they entered the church, she glanced at her closest friends, her insides pulsated with nerves. Over a thousand miles ago, the idea appeared so perfect. Now here, her stomach quivered and popped like firewood crackling in a fireplace.

"Hey, we're getting married," she said to the others as they walked into the vestibule of the town's only church. "This is what we wanted."

From what she'd seen of Angel Creek, it was a side street compared to the city of Charleston.

Walking into the sanctuary, a group of four men stood like handsome vultures peering at them as they strode through the door. Oh no, which man had gotten cold feet? Which one of them would no longer have a man to wed?

As she gazed over the viral looking men, Charity wondered which one was her man. One in particular caught her attention, his sapphire eyes dancing with amusement, his dark hair curled on his forehead as his look ensnared and held hers.

Swallowing the lump in her throat, she hoped this man would call her name.

One by one, the men's hands shook as they looked down at a paper they held and called out the women's names.

"Charity Kingston," the man said staring at her. Her heart leaped into her chest and she smiled, relief spreading through her.

The way he gazed at her sent a shiver up her spine. The man was rugged looking, and yet, his sapphire eyes twinkled with delight. And she was marrying him. With trembling knees, she walked to his side.

"Hi," he said, mischief glimmering like a beacon to his gaze. "Jakob Lewis Huntington, but my friends call me Lewis."

"Charity Kingston," she said watching him, wondering if he was a good man and what kind of husband he would be.

"Would you like to get married?"

The way he joked about what they were about to do made her smile and eased the tightly strung tension that engulfed her. "Maybe," she teased. "If you're what I'm looking for in a husband."

"Tell me what you're searching for?"

Why did she have the feeling he would agree with whatever she said, just to make her happy. Just to ease his loneliness and to marry her.

"An honest man who will never hurt me or our children and support and love me until I leave this earth."

"I'd kill any man who ever hit or harmed my wife or our babies. As your husband, it's my job to support you and our family."

Somehow she believed him. The man was confident and she trusted he would watch over her and their family. Without knowing him, she felt certain he was being truthful.

"What do you want in a wife?"

"You, darling," he said, his mouth turning up in a grin.

His words filled her with warmth and she pushed back her red hair. "When Reverend Tilly is ready, I think we should say I do."

He smiled at her and moved closer. "I thought you would never say yes."

Her husband-to-be might be a corker. She liked the way he made her feel more relaxed about taking a leap of faith and hitching their wagons together for eternity.

The back door of the building blew open and a deep, gruff voice spoke from the back of the sanctuary. "I'm here."

A huge bear of a man covered in dust hurried down to the front where they waited. With a look, he stood beside Anna and she heard him whisper something to her. All five women now had grooms.

The reverend stepped up to the altar and stared at the couples. Charity's heart began to race. This was her wedding. Not the fancy one she dreamed of as a little girl, but a simple ceremony with her friends.

The war had ended her childhood fantasies, but at this moment, she knew fate had led them to this beautiful mountain town.

"A nasty-looking storm is rushing toward Angel Creek. Before the worst of the snowfall arrives, I want everyone safe and warm in their homes. Therefore, the ceremonies will be short and simultaneous," the reverend said.

That was fine with Charity. Together the girls had survived the war and would now face married life at each other's sides. It was fitting they would all wed at the same time.

"Dearly beloved, we are gathered..." Reverend Tilly began.

Charity stared at the man she met fewer than ten minutes ago. Oh my, they would be tied together forever.

CHAPTER 3

*L*ewis was shocked. In the months since he arrived in town and taken over the saloon as Jakob Lewis Huntington, his life had changed for the better. Being a business owner, talking to the patrons, trying to be a good member of the small community, he enjoyed his new role.

A wife? Sure Lewis thought about getting married before. Once he was engaged, but today a wedding wasn't on his schedule. This afternoon when Joe came running in to tell him the brides had arrived, Lewis stared in confusion. After several moments, he understood what was going on.

Jakob's father surprised his son by ordering a mail-order bride. After she traveled thousands of miles to reach Lewis, he didn't have the heart to tell Charity he didn't want a woman.

Not wanting to draw attention to himself and his situation, he simply married the girl.

The woman's luscious red curls and expressive green eyes had tantalized him from the moment they met, and now here they were man and wife.

What else could he do, besides confess? And he hoped the

gift Jakob gave him never went away. In fact, his plan was for Jakob to repay his father and obtain the deed.

That would take time. Eventually, he might reclaim his name, but not until his own father was either dead or had given up searching for him.

After the vows were said, the women stood gazing at each other like they would never see one another again. Until finally the men took them by the hand, leading them away.

"Bye," Charity called. "I'll talk to you soon."

Tears flowed down the women's cheeks as they said their farewells, leaving the church.

"Let's go," he said.

Picking up his new wife's satchel, he took her by the arm as they hurried down the street. Snowflakes swirled around them, casting an icy halo of Angel Creek. He peeked a quick glance at the fiery red-haired woman, her green eyes wide as she bit her full lips.

The ceremony had been short and sweet. Now that her friends had left, the realization of what she'd agreed to appeared to ride her like a cowboy on a wild bull.

Kind of like agreeing to go into the military academy and once there, wondering what he was doing amongst all those high society sons. These men thought they were above the illegitimate son of a general. With scandal attached to his name, they didn't even like him.

Walking along the street, she appeared nervous, and for a moment, he thought she might run. Somehow he needed to put her at ease.

"How was your trip?"

"Long," she said. "The Missouri River tried to freeze and we feared we wouldn't make it. But here we are."

"That must have been a hard journey. I'm from--" he stopped. Lewis was raised in New York. Jakob's family resided in California and owned several large hotels that made them wealthy. How much should he tell his wife about his assumed persona?

"California," he told her, hating to lie to the woman, but knowing until he had the deed to the saloon, he would remain Jakob Huntington.

"Lucky you. You missed all the destruction from the war," she said, her voice turning sad.

No, he was right there in the midst of the fighting. For most of the great fight, his platoon had been in the middle of some of the biggest battles. Something he never wanted to experience again.

"Not really," he said. "In the military, I served under General Grant. You're right, the carnage and the lives lost were such a waste."

She gave him a sideways glance. "My father was a Confederate general. You fought for the Union?"

What would she do when and if she ever learned that his father was Union General Winfred Scott? What would she think about him then? Not that the man claimed him off the battlefield.

"Yes," he said. "Suffered a bullet wound in the Nashville battle in December last year. Walked away from the war after that. After witnessing so many men dying, I decided it was time to head west away from the insanity."

"My father must be rolling over in his grave. I'm married to a Union soldier."

This had to be settled right away or it would be a problem that would eat at their marriage. The snow continued to fall and he stopped in the center of the street. "No, you're married to Jakob Lewis Huntington, just a man trying to make a living."

A frown crossed her beautiful face, her emerald eyes serious. "Let's promise each other we will never argue over the war."

Relief rushed through him and he reached out and brushed several snowflakes from her cheeks. A surge of warmth filled him at the touch of her delicate skin and he inhaled her sweet scent.

"Agreed. The time has come to rebuild. Come on, we're almost there. I'm sure you're starving. Though I may call you my red-headed confederate rebel."

"Not a rebel, just a woman grateful to have survived."

Like she'd been struck, she jerked back. "Did you see that?"

"What?" he asked glancing around, fearful someone was sneaking up on them.

"A young boy stared at us from behind a building and when he saw me looking at him, he ran away."

"Probably young Isaac," he said. "No one has been able to catch him. We're not sure but think he's an orphan."

Staring down the alley, she frowned. "I hope he has some place warm to sleep tonight and not outdoors."

Watching her, he realized she seemed genuinely concerned about the young man. "Come on, let's get you inside. From your looks, you must be starving."

"Are you saying I'm skinny?"

"There's not much meat on your bones," he said, thinking her curves were all in the right places.

"A nice warm drink would be wonderful. Montana is a little colder than Charleston."

Taking her hand, he placed it in the crook of his arm. Yes, they were strangers, but now they were married strangers for better or worse. Charity appeared a pleasant woman, and maybe together, they could build his business into something worthwhile. At least for thirty days.

Standing in the road, she gazed at him, her teeth chattering. "Do you celebrate Christmas? Are you going to expect me to cook?"

They had so much to learn about one another. The middle of Main Street in a blizzard was not the place to find out each other's deep, dark secrets. They weren't far from his apartment.

"Yes, and yes," he said. "You're freezing, let's get you inside and get you warmed up."

While he was thinking of her, he also wanted out of the cold. Feeling began to disappear in his toes as they reached the end of the street and turned toward the saloon.

In her eyes, he could see confusion as she gave a nervous swallow. "Where are we going? There's the sheriff's office, the saloon and a bath house. Where do you live?"

Doing his best to ease her anxiety, he smiled. "Above the Angel Palace Saloon."

Like a dog on a leash, her heels dug into the snow, coming to a halt and almost caused them to slip and fall. "The saloon?"

"Yes," he said proudly. Until he purchased the saloon, he liked to think of it as being Jakob's and he managed the business. One day he would purchase the business and the Angel Palace would belong to him.

"No, I can't live above a saloon."

"Why not?" he asked, stunned.

Turning to him, her mouth opened. "It's not a..."

With a questioning glance at her, he didn't understand what she was trying to say. Yet her cheeks turned a bright shade of rose making her even more beautiful. Why didn't the bachelors in Charleston snatch her up?

Suddenly he understood what she was saying and began to laugh. The woman must be an innocent.

"There is no brothel in town. We sell liquor and some food. Not even gambling or card playing."

"My husband owns a saloon," she said, staring at the sign. "Alcohol is the devil's brew."

"This is how I make our living," he said, wondering why in the world Jakob's father had thought the boy needed a woman. Then again, Jakob had made some really poor choices in life.

"Didn't you know you were marrying the saloon owner?"

"No, I did not," she said.

The urge to retort *at least she knew she was getting hitched—* which was more than his own knowledge--burned strongly, but he resisted.

"Well, honey, it's a little late. Do you want to back out? Is that what you want to do?"

A lost look appeared in her gaze. A haunted stare only the war could have created. An empty look that he'd seen on dozens of victims that let him know she experienced loss during the great conflict.

A gust of wind blew snow against his face, the freezing pellets biting.

"Here we are," he said, standing in the street outside his business. At first, he'd been shocked at how nice the saloon was, but now he enjoyed making the place his own. "The Angel Palace."

"Should you use the name Angel on a house of drinking," she said.

"That's the name of the town."

"Why palace?"

What should he say?

"The original owner called it The Angel Palace and I just left it."

This time next year when he had the rightful papers, he would change the name to something that didn't sound so wimpy. A more manly drinking name. The Angel Palace sounded like a dance hall where women entertained themselves and all he had was a skinny barmaid.

Now with a wife, he was certain his rebel teetotaler would never agree to Hurdy Gurdy girls in the saloon. What self-respecting woman would want her husband owning a dance hall?

When they reached the outer doors, he turned to her and smiled. "The boys would be disappointed if I didn't carry you over the threshold."

The wind howled louder. "What?"

"Never mind," he said and scooped her up in his arms before she had a chance to object.

"Oh," she cried as he carried her into the saloon.

The music inside came to a halt and a loud roar of approval rose from the crowd as he took Charity up the stairs to his apartment.

The woman weighed very little and yet through her bulky warm clothes, he could feel a soft round ass. As she looped her arms around his neck, he glanced at her flawless face. With those saucy green eyes and lashes that appeared dipped in red with tips of gold, she must be Irish.

The woman smelled heavenly. Maybe today had been his lucky day to gain such a beautiful creature for his wife.

Opening the door to the small apartment, he stepped inside and closed the door. Setting his bride down, he said, "Welcome home."

STANDING INSIDE THE SMALL APARTMENT, she gazed around at the simple furnishings. A small parlor held a sofa and chair. A dinner table with two chairs and a wood-burning stove in the corner not only heated the room, but must also serve as the cook stove. In the back, a room with a bed.

A large frightening bed that had tremors of fear cascading through her. "Only one bedroom?"

As he sat her satchel on the ground next to her, he rose and glanced at her. "That's it."

"The contract said we would not sleep together for thirty days, so we can annul the marriage if either of us wants out."

With a shrug he said, "With only one bed, you can take the couch."

"I'm your wife; you wouldn't give me the bed?"

"No, as I have to work all day and most of the night. My job may not seem physical, but lifting crates of whiskey can be heavy. I need a good night's rest."

It was bad enough her husband was a saloon owner, but there was only one bed in the apartment and he declined to give it up. At least he didn't own a brothel and the memory of the torn dress and the inside of the house wrecked made her smile. Irish women did not like to be insulted or given ultimatums. John Roberts III received a schooling in the proper way to treat a woman.

Staring at the man, she thought maybe he needed a lesson in Irish manners. It was conventional for a man to give the woman the only sleeping quarters. But her husband refused.

Until she made up her mind if she could stay with a saloon owner, she would not share a bed with Lewis.

"I'll take the couch," she said, biting her lip, knowing she had to say her piece. "As your wife, I don't want any liquor in our home."

The man grinned at her, his smile causing dimples to appear on his cheeks. His blue eyes twinkled, and that sly grin sent a delicious tremor down her spine. The combination was a mischievous look that already she recognized.

"Honey, all the alcohol is downstairs. No need to keep any up here."

"Great, just remember liquor goes against my code of ethics as a Christian woman."

"Understand," he said, walking to stand in front of her. His finger touched her cheek and trailed down to her lips, leaving a trail of heat as she gasped. "There are plenty of Christian men in my establishment every night. And there are always a couple of trouble makers and then the drunks. Those are the ones I would like to bar from the building, but it's a small town and every person puts food on our table."

Until the blasted war, food and a roof over her head were never a concern. With the great conflict, everything changed.

"Now, why don't I heat us up some chili and we'll sit down and have our first dinner together," he said. "You can help me in the kitchen."

"I've never eaten chili."

"Then you've got to try it."

She bit her lip, not certain she wanted to reveal that until a year ago, when their last servant fled in the middle of the night, she had never cooked anything in her life. A respectable southern woman had servants who prepared the meals and cleaned her house. Not anymore.

"My cooking is not the best. Until recently, I never had to prepare a meal. When you're hungry, you learn very quickly how to cook."

A feeling of warmth overcame her. What would happen tonight, she didn't know, but he appeared not to be pushing her in any direction she didn't want to go and that made her feel better. The thought of sleeping with a strange man left her terrified and yet, Lewis was making no demands.

"Have you ever made cornbread?" he asked.

"No," she said, walking into the food prep area. Compared to the kitchen in their home in Charleston this was a mere closet. Pain gripped her heart.

That was no longer her home and was instead a gentleman's club. Before departing, she hoped they enjoyed the mess she created just for them. Plus, a letter about ghosts haunting the house should make the owner a little nervous. Not that there were spirits, but he didn't need to know that.

"Let's make it together," he said, pulling out containers of flour and cornmeal from cabinets.

She watched as he measured out the ingredients. From a wooden box, he pulled a bottle of milk and she stared at him in surprise. "How did you keep that cool?"

"Twice a day, I pack the box with snow. Or a chunk of ice if any is available and it keeps everything inside chilled," he said. "During the war, I learned this trick."

"Oh," she said. "Our servants always took care of keeping the food in the basement iced. I've never had to worry about such things before."

While he whipped the ingredients, he stared at her, his blue eyes studying her. "Did your family own one of those fancy plantation homes I saw."

The memories came flooding back and she longed for the drawings of the house sitting on Elizabeth Street. The grand old mansion. But the art would not fit in her trunk.

"No, but we had a nice house. My father was a merchant and did quite well. Unfortunately, he put all of his money into the confederacy who assured us they would win. What a waste."

That was in the past and this was her life now. Though she would miss the easy lifestyle she'd grown up with, thank goodness, she wasn't working in a whorehouse.

"Any brothers or sisters?"

"My brother was killed at the battle of Gettysburg."

"Your family gave a lot to the war. A father and a brother," he said. "That must be tough."

"We suffered just like everyone else. Some families lost more than we did," she said, greasing a pan for the cornbread. "What about your family?"

"I'm the only child my mother ever had," he said. "She's long gone, though my father is still alive."

"Where does he live?"

"California," he replied.

"Is that where you grew up?"

"No, as a kid I lived in New York."

"My favorite town," she said. "On my twelfth birthday, Papa took us to see the city. Why did you move to California? Seems so far."

For a moment, he didn't say anything as he looked away and put the chili into a pan and placed it on the stove. "My father's business."

"Oh, did you like living there?"

"No," he said, his back to her as he stirred the food.

For a man who had been open and honest with her, it seemed like a door had slammed shut. Turning to her, he offered her a spoonful. "Taste it and tell me if you like it."

Holding the spoon to her lips, she opened her mouth. Mere inches separated him from her and she moaned at the texture of the meat. "Delicious."

The savoriness ignited her hunger as she licked her lips and he moved even closer.

"Since the ceremony, I've wanted another kiss."

Once again, his lips covered hers and the caress of his mouth ripped her breath away. Oh no, what would he want next?

STANDING INSIDE THE SMALL APARTMENT, she gazed around at the simple furnishings. A small parlor held a sofa and chair. A dinner table with two chairs and a wood-burning stove in the corner not only heated the room, but must also serve as the cook stove. In the back, a room with a bed.

A large frightening bed that had tremors of fear cascading through her. "Only one bedroom?"

As he sat her satchel on the ground next to her, he rose and glanced at her. "That's it."

"The contract said we would not sleep together for thirty days, so we can annul the marriage if either of us wants out."

With a shrug he said, "With only one bed, you can take the couch."

"I'm your wife; you wouldn't give me the bed?"

"No, as I have to work all day and most of the night. My job may not seem physical, but lifting crates of whiskey can be heavy. I need a good night's rest."

It was bad enough her husband was a saloon owner, but there was only one bed in the apartment and he declined to give it up. At least he didn't own a brothel and the memory of the torn dress and the inside of the house wrecked made her smile. Irish women did not like to be insulted or given ultimatums. John Roberts III received a schooling in the proper way to treat a woman.

Staring at the man, she thought maybe he needed a lesson in Irish manners. It was conventional for a man to give the woman the only sleeping quarters. But her husband refused.

Until she made up her mind if she could stay with a saloon owner, she would not share a bed with Lewis.

"I'll take the couch," she said, biting her lip, knowing she had to say her piece. "As your wife, I don't want any liquor in our home."

The man grinned at her, his smile causing dimples to appear on his cheeks. His blue eyes twinkled, and that sly grin sent a delicious tremor down her spine. The combination was a mischievous look that already she recognized.

"Honey, all the alcohol is downstairs. No need to keep any up here."

"Great, just remember liquor goes against my code of ethics as a Christian woman."

"Understand," he said, walking to stand in front of her. His finger touched her cheek and trailed down to her lips, leaving a trail of heat as she gasped. "There are plenty of Christian men in my establishment every night. And there are always a couple of trouble makers and then the drunks. Those are the ones I would like to bar from the building, but it's a small town and every person puts food on our table."

Until the blasted war, food and a roof over her head were never a concern. With the great conflict, everything changed.

"Now, why don't I heat us up some chili and we'll sit down and have our first dinner together," he said. "You can help me in the kitchen."

"I've never eaten chili."

"Then you've got to try it."

She bit her lip, not certain she wanted to reveal that until a year ago, when their last servant fled in the middle of the night, she had never cooked anything in her life. A respectable southern woman had servants who prepared the meals and cleaned her house. Not anymore.

"My cooking is not the best. Until recently, I never had to prepare a meal. When you're hungry, you learn very quickly how to cook."

A feeling of warmth overcame her. What would happen tonight, she didn't know, but he appeared not to be pushing her in any direction she didn't want to go and that made her feel better. The thought of sleeping with a strange man left her terrified and yet, Lewis was making no demands.

"Have you ever made cornbread?" he asked.

"No," she said, walking into the food prep area. Compared to the kitchen in their home in Charleston this was a mere closet. Pain gripped her heart.

That was no longer her home and was instead a gentleman's club. Before departing, she hoped they enjoyed the mess she created just for them. Plus, a letter about ghosts haunting the house should make the owner a little nervous. Not that there were spirits, but he didn't need to know that.

"Let's make it together," he said, pulling out containers of flour and cornmeal from cabinets.

She watched as he measured out the ingredients. From a wooden box, he pulled a bottle of milk and she stared at him in surprise. "How did you keep that cool?"

"Twice a day, I pack the box with snow. Or a chunk of ice if any is available and it keeps everything inside chilled," he said. "During the war, I learned this trick."

"Oh," she said. "Our servants always took care of keeping the food in the basement iced. I've never had to worry about such things before."

While he whipped the ingredients, he stared at her, his blue eyes studying her. "Did your family own one of those fancy plantation homes I saw."

The memories came flooding back and she longed for the drawings of the house sitting on Elizabeth Street. The grand old mansion. But the art would not fit in her trunk.

"No, but we had a nice house. My father was a merchant and did quite well. Unfortunately, he put all of his money into the confederacy who assured us they would win. What a waste."

That was in the past and this was her life now. Though she would miss the easy lifestyle she'd grown up with, thank goodness, she wasn't working in a whorehouse.

"Any brothers or sisters?"

"My brother was killed at the battle of Gettysburg."

"Your family gave a lot to the war. A father and a brother," he said. "That must be tough."

"We suffered just like everyone else. Some families lost more than we did," she said, greasing a pan for the cornbread. "What about your family?"

"I'm the only child my mother ever had," he said. "She's long gone, though my father is still alive."

"Where does he live?"

"California," he replied.

"Is that where you grew up?"

"No, as a kid I lived in New York."

"My favorite town," she said. "On my twelfth birthday, Papa took us to see the city. Why did you move to California? Seems so far."

For a moment, he didn't say anything as he looked away and

put the chili into a pan and placed it on the stove. "My father's business."

"Oh, did you like living there?"

"No," he said, his back to her as he stirred the food.

For a man who had been open and honest with her, it seemed like a door had slammed shut. Turning to her, he offered her a spoonful. "Taste it and tell me if you like it."

Holding the spoon to her lips, she opened her mouth. Mere inches separated him from her and she moaned at the texture of the meat. "Delicious."

The savoriness ignited her hunger as she licked her lips and he moved even closer.

"Since the ceremony, I've wanted another kiss."

Once again, his lips covered hers and the caress of his mouth ripped her breath away. Oh no, what would he want next?

~

LEWIS LONGED to kiss her since that first peck in the church. That smooch had been just a sealing of their vows and commitments to one another.

This kiss...this kiss sent his blood rushing to the center of his body like a wild horse charging across the prairie. Like a bull rider holding on for dear life as he rode that hunk of pure raging terror. Like a lion roaring in the jungle, proclaiming he was king. Lewis was shocked at his body's reaction.

The feel of her full lips beneath his, soft and resilient, as he pulled her against his chest, her breasts snug. Just when things began to get heated, he heard the chili boiling over.

Reluctantly, he released her and turned back to the stove and stirred the sauce. When he whirled back to her, she stood mesmerized. Her emerald eyes large, held his gaze as she stared at him in shock, her hand touching her lips.

Oh yes, that kiss affected her the same as him. A smile radiated from his face and he laid his hand on her arm. "Are you ready to eat?"

"Uh, yes," she said, shaking her head like she was breaking the spell.

"How many other women have you kissed like that?" she said suddenly surprising him.

"Not many, one maybe two," he said, thinking she didn't need to worry about anyone else. "Before the war, I was engaged, but when that ended, there hasn't been another woman since then."

"Why didn't you marry her?"

"Wasn't meant to be," he said, dishing up bowls of the soup. Someday he would tell her about Scarlet, but that was a Lewis story and Jakob was on this side of the country during that time. Once the saloon was in Lewis name, if they were still married, he would tell her everything. "My fiancée didn't want me. I wasn't good enough."

It was partially the truth. Once she found out he was illegitimate, she broke off their engagement. Until today, he'd forgotten all about his debutante fiancée.

Charity took the cornbread out of the oven and put it on the stove. They sat at the small rectangular table just big enough for two.

"I guess you don't entertain often," she said.

"No, there's been no reason for anyone to visit. Something tells me those ladies you arrived with will be over often."

The mention of the other girls brought a smile to her face. "We've been friends for a long time."

The memory of military school and being ostracized left him cringing inside. Because of his birth, he never had any close friends. Once they learned he was a bastard, no one wanted to be associated with him.

"So, tell me why you became a mail-order bride?"

With interest, he watched the expressions on her face before she lifted her chin, determination in her gaze. Strength oozed from his wife and from the fiery red curls to flashing green eyes, he would never want to cross her.

"After the war, there was no money for me to pay the taxes. So, the house was auctioned off."

"A carpet bagger purchased it?" he asked.

Charity took a dainty bite of her chili and then it appeared she couldn't stop. The woman had been starving. Finally, she slowed down.

"No, a brothel owner."

Stunned, Lewis stared at her. "What did you do?"

"That's when I saw the ad in the Groom's Gazette and I told my friends. So few young men had returned home and the area was so depressing. With the reconstruction, it seemed like the perfect time to leave."

For some reason, he felt there was bit more to this story, like she only gave him the highlights she wanted him to know.

Familiar with the type of men who operated a whorehouse, Lewis knew the man tried to influence his beautiful wife to work for him. A thousand miles separated them and that was a good thing. Never would there be a house of ill repute attached to his business.

"Here we are," she said, moaning as she bit into the cornbread. "This is so good."

Watching her, the way she scarfed down her food, he realized she hadn't eaten in some time.

"How long has it been since you ate?"

A quick glance and he could see she knew he'd been staring at her. "Two days."

A rush of fury rippled along his spine. Did she have no money at all? This was how women like her were trapped into prostitution and all kinds of bad things.

"Why didn't you eat?"

With a contented sigh, she pushed her red curls off her

shoulder and gave a quiet womanly burp. "With very little cash between us, I made certain the other girls didn't go hungry."

"Do you have *any* money?"

Biting her lip, she stared at him sheepishly, and he knew. A fierce protectiveness overcame him.

"No," she said softly.

"Tomorrow we will go down to the bank and add you to my account. Afterwards, we'll go over to the mercantile so you can make purchases and put it on my bill. I'll give you five dollars a week spending money. Don't ever leave this house without cash."

Her mouth fell open and she stared at him, her eyes large. "Are we rich?"

Unable to contain his laughter, Lewis threw back his head and laughed. "No, we're not rich by any means, but the saloon makes a nice living and I don't want my wife walking around without money. Do you understand?"

With a nod, she smiled remembering happier times. "My Papa would become so mad at me and my mother for leaving the house without money. Mother and I charged everything on his accounts and never worried about the amount. That was before the war. That was before we lost everything."

Obviously, his wife came from wealth and the conflict must have been extremely hard on her. Going from a life of luxury to poverty had surely taught her so many life lessons, not all of them good. The thought of her traveling across country with little or no money left him angrier. But what were her other choices?

"We can't go overboard, but you can purchase things we need for the house and groceries. Tomorrow we're going to get you a warm pair of boots and a heavy coat. Yours is not heavy enough."

"Thank you." She bit her lip in that enticing way that made him want to place his hands on her and move his mouth over her lips once again. As he gazed at her, it took a herculean effort, but he restrained himself.

"Tell me why you ordered a mail-order bride? Why couldn't you find some girl here in town to marry you?"

Just the sort of question he never considered because he didn't order a bride. Only his pretend father could answer why he requested Jakob a wife. Lewis was the man on the receiving end.

Eventually, Lewis planned on getting married, but not at this moment. Sometimes life gave you a gift you couldn't deny. Jakob Huntington had now given him two wonderful gifts. If only Jakob's father and his own stayed away long enough for him to earn enough to buy the saloon, things would be great.

"I'm fairly new to town and I've been lonely. The war took any chance of me finding someone in New York and there is a shortage of women here in Angel Creek. So here you are."

Every time he lied to her, his stomach churned and ached. Disgust radiating like a plague through him as he hated lying and liars. How quickly he was becoming one.

He couldn't wait for the day when he could be honest with her.

"And you got me. A woman who can't cook, barely cleans house, but throws a delightful tea party or quilting event. Anything to do with needlework."

Reaching out he took her hand. "You'll learn. Life has dealt both of us a tremendous change since the war. We're learning all over again and we'll get it right."

She squeezed his hand. "Possibly even a family of our own."

The thought paralyzed him for a moment. With a wife came babies, children, and mouths to feed. Yet the idea also excited him.

"Guess the saloon better start earning more money."

"First, we have to decide if we want to remain married. Thirty days."

A groan escaped him. Thirty days of her sleeping on the couch, of being around her, of smelling, touching her, but no relations in the marital bed. His wife was making it clear, no hanky-panky for the next month. The man in him screamed no. You're her husband, do it.

•

CHAPTER 4

*T*hat night after they washed the dinner dishes, she went to her reticule and then glanced back at him. Never had she undressed before a man. In fact, this small cramped apartment was going to make it very difficult for privacy. "When will the driver deliver my trunk?"

"It's probably downstairs. Do you need something?"

"No, I have everything I need here. I just wanted to make certain the trunk arrived after we left in such a rush."

The way he gazed at her left her nervous. Like he longed to kiss her again and again and while the idea was tantalizing, she feared where it would lead. "Why don't I go down and find your luggage while you get ready for bed."

Relief flooded her as the thought of disrobing in front of her husband had her as jumpy as a panther in the dark. He walked out the door, leaving her alone and she sighed, knowing this was her life.

Quickly, she grabbed her nightgown. The fabric had once been so pretty, but now the garment was worn and appeared bare in places. Maybe when he gave her the allowance, she would splurge. The door suddenly opened and she whirled around giving him her back while she wrapped her wrapper around herself.

"Brought your trunk up in case you needed it," he said dropping it on the floor.

"Thanks," she said, whirling back around with her robe securely tied, her heart pounding at how he almost caught her in her nightclothes. Sure, she knew eventually they would see each other, but she wasn't ready. Six hours was not enough time for her to adjust to this new life and bare herself to him.

Licking his lips, he stared at her. "The first few days are probably going to be challenging as we get used to living together. If you need anything at all, you come tell me. And if you don't understand my reasoning about something, talk to me."

It was hard to believe that this was her wedding night. Nothing like what she'd dreamed of with a man she loved. Never would she have imagined as a young child, she would become a mail-order bride and wed a man she just met.

Everything seemed awkward and yet with her parents, she never witnessed any stiltedness between them. Then again, they were married for years before she came into their lives.

"My parents had a wonderful marriage. Theirs has always been the kind of relationship I wanted to have, but I'm sure they didn't start out that way. It must have taken years."

Taking her into his arms, he held her for a moment and she liked the comfort of his embrace. "We'll take it slow."

Releasing her, he turned his nose up at the couch. "You're sure you want to sleep on that sofa?"

Biting her lip, she longed to change her mind. That bed looked so inviting, especially after the days of rattling around inside a stagecoach. But she couldn't lie with a man she didn't know, even if they had said *I do*.

"I'll take the sofa."

"Okay, let me find you a pillow and blanket."

While she waited, she looked around at the small apartment, thinking this would be her home. The furnishings were functional at best. With a little needlework and a little money, she would turn this into a cute place to live. That had to wait until tomorrow. Tonight, she was so exhausted, she could barely keep her eyes open.

When Lewis returned, he handed her what she needed to make her bed. As he walked away, she crawled onto the couch. A spring rubbed up against her back and a bulge was beneath her hips, but she would make do. No wonder he didn't want to spend the night on this antiquated lump of stuffed material.

"Time for a new sofa," she said as he blew out the lantern. In the darkness, she heard him shedding his pants and shirt. A trickle of curiosity had her straining to see him in the dark. The bed creaked as he slipped under the covers.

Standing, she removed her wrapper and laid it close. Lying down on the hard divan, she groaned. She could be sleeping next to him. She could be enjoying that mattress.

"Never had much need for that piece of furniture until now. The other side of the bed is empty."

The sound of a nice warm bed was so tempting, but it didn't seem right. "Goodnight, Lewis."

"Goodnight, Charity. Happy wedding night."

A giggle erupted from between her lips, her nerves overwhelming her of how she would remember and tell their children of their first night together. The night the bride gave herself to the groom and yet here she was spending the night on an antique sofa.

"What's so funny?" he asked.

"Our wedding night. I'm on a lumpy divan and you're in the bed."

A moment of silence and then footsteps. Strong arms lifted her off the couch and she gasped. "What are you doing?"

"Taking my wife to bed, where she belongs."

For a second, she wanted to protest, but she was too tired to fight as she linked her arms around his neck. Walking to the opposite side, he laid her on the soft mattress.

She feared the worst, but he curled around her and kissed her neck. "Goodnight, Charity."

Unable to move, she lay there frozen, his manly parts snug against her. Yet this bed felt delightful compared to the sofa. With a sigh, she softly said, "Goodnight, Lewis."

The next morning, Charity awoke with Lewis's arms around her. Warmth surrounded her and she couldn't remember the last time she slept so soundly.

While living in that big old house, she worried about sleeping through someone breaking in. Many nights she spent on her mother's favorite divan in the parlor just to make certain no one had plans of stealing under the guise of darkness.

People were desperate for food and money and anything to get them through the war. And a single woman in a house that appeared opulent on the outside was a huge target. If the criminals looked on the inside, the riches were either taken by the Union army or sold to put food on the table.

Warm lips pressed along her neck, kissing her softly sending a stampede of tremors trampling down her spine.

"Good morning," he said, his deep voice resonating.

"Good morning," she responded afraid to move, yet enjoying the body heat her husband generated against her. "How do you spend your days?"

"Well, this is a new way to start my day. Waking up next to my wife is nice," he said his hand rubbing up and down her arm, his touch creating a ripple of awareness through her.

They had just met and yet Lewis seemed to create all kinds of sensations within her when he touched her. No man, not even the boy she courted ever made her feel this way.

Her breath caught in her throat and she sighed. "What else do you do?"

"Well, normally, I cook some breakfast and then go down and stock the bar. Check to see if everything is clean and ready for tonight's crowd. Most nights, I don't come up until late. Because of our wedding, I took the evening off."

She turned onto her back and gazed at him. "Thank you. Who works for you?"

"Just me and my barmaid, Alice. She's a single mother and was looking to find a job. No one would hire her, so I did."

With few workers helping him, it must've been hard to take a night off. In her heart, she knew she would have been furious if he had worked through their wedding night. Their first night together, she wanted to learn more about her new husband. A little time with the man before they began their normal life. A chance to get to know the man.

Charity didn't want to dress in front of Lewis, so she lay there beside him wondering how she could put her clothes on without him being in the same room. Finally, she threw back the covers and ran over to the sofa where her wrapper lay.

In the cold, she hurriedly wrapped it around her, then she drew back the curtains and looked out the window.

"Oh my, there is so much snow. There's two feet and it's still coming down."

"Winter has officially arrived," he said.

Keeping her back to him, she heard the rustle of his pants and didn't dare look toward the sound.

"Let's fix breakfast together," he said. "I'll let you do the cooking and I'll stand by and watch."

"What do you want me to fix?" she asked.

"Let's start off with scrambled eggs," he said. "They're easier than fried."

Turning from the window she watched him pull out the ingredients. Soon she would know where everything was and would be the one to cook their meals. Especially with her husband working such long hours.

The saloon opened in the afternoons and went until midnight, and on the weekend, it was even later. How would she spend her time here in this room all alone? Until they had children, she didn't have that much to do.

With Lewis's help, she soon had their eggs made and as they sat at the table, she laughed. "That wasn't all that hard. I think I can make scrambled eggs by myself now."

At no time in her younger years had she imagined her life without servants. The biggest challenge, she'd discovered so far, was laundry. One of her favorite dresses bore a scorch spot because of her ineptitude with the iron. How in the world did she know you didn't leave it in the fire that long?

"Tomorrow, we'll tackle frying eggs and bacon."

Stunned, she put her fork down. "Bacon. You have bacon?"

At that instant, her mouth started watering. The thought of crisp bacon was enough to make her consider getting up and cooking it right this moment. But would she burn it like she had her dress?

"Yes," he said staring at her oddly.

"Since the war started, I haven't had bacon. We gave up our rations for the soldiers. I've forgotten what it tastes like."

There were so many things she lost in that dreadful war. The loss of her father, her brother, her mother and eventually their wealth. Never could she condone any kind of conflict again.

"Tomorrow morning we'll fry it up," he said. "After breakfast, I'll go down and work a bit in the saloon while you dress. Then we should run to the bank and the mercantile. At the mercantile, I want to buy you a better coat and some gloves. We'll establish you can use my credit and I'll give you five dollars."

Tears spring to her eyes as she stared at this very generous man. Yes, they were married, but that didn't mean he had to purchase her new clothing. "Why are you doing this? My coat is old, but it works."

Reaching across the table, he laid his hand on her wrist. "You're my wife for at least the next thirty days. Montana is cold and I want you warm."

Emotion welled up inside her at her husband's generosity. After losing everything, he was a welcome respite in the storm. If he was trying to win her heart, the man was making an excellent run for it.

When he carried her to bed last night, she feared he would make unwanted advances. Yet she fell fast asleep and this morning, she realized nothing had happened.

The man let her sleep, and for the first time in days, she felt rested.

~

LATER THAT AFTERNOON, after Lewis went to the saloon, Charity hurried across the snow covered street, trying to carefully avoid messing up her new boots. Part of her wanted to remove them and carry them in her arms, but that would defeat their purpose. After all, they were the first pair of new shoes in over four years.

When she reached the sidewalk, she stepped on to the porch of the house where Sarah lived with her husband. The sheriff would be at work in the jail and she needed to see her friend. There was so much to discuss.

White flakes still trickled down, but the storm's intensity was waning, and the skies appeared to be clearing as she stood on the steps. While being a mail-order bride may not have been what she wanted, last night and this morning had not been bad.

Getting to know Lewis who was so sweet and kind and the man kissed like the devil. And he insisted on kissing her and holding her. Just the skim of his fingers against her cheek left her hungry with an urge for things she knew nothing of and never experienced.

She still needed to talk to Sarah. She'd been married before and she understood what being with a man was like. In all her years, she never witnessed her parents kissing or her father holding her mother in an embrace. Yet their union had been a happy one or so she believed.

The war never gave Charity the opportunity to court much, and she needed guidance as to what a man expected. She had only one brief courtship before the war started, before the men left to join the fight.

Standing there, Charity nervously knocked on the door, anxious to speak with her friend.

Sarah swung open the door. "Oh my, I'm so happy to see you."

"It's only been a day. After the trip, I thought you'd be glad to be rid of me."

"No, I've missed you," Sarah told her.

The two girls gave each other a hug and Charity felt like days had passed since they'd been together.

"Come in and look at this house. Can you believe this disaster? At least, I'm here far enough away from the inlaws."

Looking around, Charity could tell the house was built well, but she had to agree with Sarah. The place was a little rough. "It's nice. You should see our place, it's one bedroom. Your man, he's treating you well?"

"Well, he's been at work. We're still learning about one another."

At least Lewis had taken their wedding night off, but a sheriff was always on the job. Always needed to be near his prisoners.

"Look, he bought me a new coat and boots and he's kind, Sarah, but I don't know how to act around him. I'm so confused as to what he expects," she said with a smile. Why did new clothes always make you feel pretty?

"Come in and tell me what you mean," Sarah said, ushering her into the house.

They walked into her parlor and Charity began to pace the floor. Of course, she knew about the marital bed, but what happened between a man and woman up to that point. What happened before you found yourself naked beside a man? Why did women whisper and giggle about their first night?

"You've been married before. What do I do? Do I let him watch me undress? Do I let him kiss me?"

Her friend looked at her like she was crazy. "Take a deep breath and calm down. You're having bridal jitters. Right now, you're getting to know one another, and hopefully, he doesn't expect anything from you in bed."

The memory of how he only held her came to mind. Waking up in his arms left her warm and filled with wonder. The press of his body against hers sent frightened butterflies scurrying through her. Exciting and terrifying, all at once. "Last night we stayed in the same bed together."

Sarah's hazel eyes widened. "You didn't..."

Still pacing the room, she shook her head emphatically. "No. No, but the apartment is small. The bed is right off the main room and there's a tiny kitchen area. The apartment is smaller than our kitchen back home."

Memories of living in luxury weren't doing her any favors. The past needed to stay in the past and she needed to move on to the future.

"Why didn't he sleep on the sofa?"

"Believe me, I tried. But that couch is a horrible piece of furniture, and well, he carried me to bed and told me to close my eyes. In his arms, warmth and security lulled me right to sleep. The last time I slept so soundly was before the war, and nothing happened between us."

Sarah's brows rose as she stared at her friend. "Did you want something to happen?"

Sure she was curious about *that*, but if they had joined last night, the act would've had no meaning. There were no feelings of love between them. Together they were each serving a need for the other and she needed to remind herself of that fact.

"No, but the man's kisses are divine, and this morning, I awoke in his arms with him pressing his mouth along the back of my neck. Am I supposed to experience tremors or strange tingles racing down my spine when his hand brushes mine?"

"That's wonderful." Laughing, Sarah placed her hand over her mouth. "Sh....Becca is down for a nap and I don't want to wake her. Your husband is a good match for you. Be careful."

"This morning he demanded that we go to the mercantile so I could purchase what I need. And he's giving me a five-dollar allowance every week. Five dollars. Twenty dollars a month for me to do whatever I want."

Until the war started, she never worried about money. Whenever she needed something, she purchased what she wanted and her father paid for it. All of that ended when the confederate money became worthless.

Finally, Charity sat next to her friend. "Yesterday, I was so scared, but this morning we cooked breakfast together and then we went to the bank and he added me on all his accounts."

Sarah reached out and laid her hand on Charity's arm. "He's making room in his life for you. To me, it sounds like he wishes for a real union and he's doing everything he can to make certain that happens. What he wants from you? Men want sex, and like us, they want children and love and affection. Does he touch you a lot?"

Charity felt her cheeks flame at the way he seemed to always touch or simply was near her. Like he wanted to be next to her, no matter where they went.

"Constantly. Either his hand is at my side, my elbow, or he

reaches across the table and caresses my hand."

"The man is courting you. Unfortunately, the war kept you from being courted much and this is kind of how it is. A man touches you to assure you he cares and to show the world you're his. Do you like him?"

Did she like him? Oh yes, she not only liked the man, but deemed Lewis her knight in shining armor. Yet, she was afraid. At least, so far in her life, nothing remained permanent. Everything was fleeting and she feared Lewis would not be in her life for long. Then there was his business.

"My only problem is he owns the Angel Creek Palace. Our apartment is above the saloon. As you know, my parents were very strict and my mother never allowed alcohol in our home. She called it the devil's brew. Now I'm the saloon owner's wife," she said, still not sure if she could accept his occupation.

"Times have changed for everyone," Sarah said. "Just as long as he's not a drunk, and he continues to support you, you'll be fine."

"How do I please him?" she asked, knowing she really did want to make him happy. If they hadn't consummated their marriage, either one of them could ask for an annulment in the first thirty days. What if her husband changed his mind?

"Honey, I wish I knew. Remember, I was the bride whose husband cheated on her. I'm searching for answers myself."

"We're cooking together, so he can show me how," Charity said, thinking back to this morning when they had made scrambled eggs.

"The only advice I was ever given was men need to think they rule their little kingdom and then they will make you their queen," she said with a laugh. "Only with my first husband, he forgot the queen part."

Was she making something out of nothing? Was she overreacting to the end of a long journey with the obvious outcome when she arrived, she wanted to turn and run.

Glancing at her friend, she realized she had been completely selfish focusing on herself. "Thank you. You calmed me down, as I was so overwhelmed when I came in here. But what about you? How was your night? Did you like your man?"

With a heavy sigh, Sarah said, "My man came home and promptly went to work. Someone has to stay with the locked-up men. Most of the time, he's been gone. Becca and I spent the night in his bed. Actually, it was nice as the two of us unpacked and relaxed. She's sleeping now."

The sound of little feet running barefoot across a wooden floor drew their attention. "Hi, baby," Sarah said picking up her daughter and putting her in her lap. "Did you have a nice nap?"

The precocious child gave her mother a look that most debutantes worked to perfect. A lifting of the brows and then a haughty stare.

"Big girls don't take naps. I didn't sleep. I just rested my eyes."

Smiling, Charity touched the little girl's golden curls. "Becca, the entire time we were on that stagecoach, you kept me entertained."

The little girl's mouth puckered in a frown. "Don't want to go back on coach."

Sarah kissed the top of her daughter's head. "Me either, honey. Me either."

"Want to see Grandma and Grandpa."

"Not today," Sarah said, an intense look in her eyes that any mother trying to protect their child would recognize. Charity admired her friend for how she fiercely fought for her daughter and in the end outwitted the devious in-laws.

With a quick glance around to make sure the sheriff had not returned, Charity asked, "Do you think we made the right decision?"

"We made the only choice we could. Time will tell if it was right."

CHAPTER 5

*I*n the week since they married, Charity made it a habit to pop into the saloon and see her husband hard at work. She found herself bored in their small apartment. After Lewis left for the saloon, she unpacked and rearranged and made the place a little more homey with some of her own touches.

Still there was nothing for her to do and she was beginning to go stir crazy. Finally, one evening when she took down his supper, with shock, she noticed him trying to do all the tasks. "What happened to your barmaid?"

"Her son is running a fever and I told her to go home to him," he said, pouring whiskey into glasses and rushing off to serve them.

When he returned, she said, "What can I do to help?"

A frown appeared on his face and his brows drew together and his mouth turned down. "Before you said you wanted nothing to do with the saloon."

At first, she had been adamant about never traipsing into a place that served alcohol. Until she realized because of this business, she once again had a roof over her head and food to eat. Whenever she came down, the saloon was busy with men mainly sitting anf talking. Some played darts while others drank whiskey. Not the wild place she imagined.

"Maybe I've changed my mind," she said. "You need the help, and frankly, I need something to keep me from running out of the building bored out of my mind."

Doubt reflected from his gaze as he leaned back and stared at her like he wasn't quite certain. "Let's try it tonight, but if any of the men give you any trouble, you tell me."

Warmth suffused her at the way he wanted to protect her. The more she knew about Lewis Huntington, the more she liked the man. No, they hadn't met in the traditional way, but so far Lewis fulfilled all her expectations. Plus, every time he gazed at her, her insides melted into a puddle.

"Okay, tell me what I need to do."

"These drinks go to table one. When you get back from that table, I'll have another tray ready for you."

"Do I need to collect the money?"

"Yes," he said. "Five cents a shot or twenty-five cents for the bottle."

Picking up the tray, Charity walked over to the table.

"'Bout time you arrived," a man said, pushing back his hat and gazing at her. "Never seen you before."

"I'm married to Lewis," she said. "Sorry about the delay, our barmaid's son is ill."

The man frowned. "That's a damn shame. Don't seem fair a man like him has a woman like you."

That one she needed to stay away from. The idea of a man with an unkempt beard and a dirty face, drinking whiskey, touching her, made her shiver with revulsion.

"Twenty-five cents," she said, setting the bottle down along with the glasses.

The man counted out thirty cents. "Keep the change."

Oh my, he gave her a nickel. Lewis never mentioned

tips. The thought of poor Alice at home with a sick child, earning nothing left her sad. Charity was the lucky one with an allowance and a husband to take care of her. Alice had no one.

"Thank you, sir," she said and turned away hurrying back to the bar where she took another tray.

"Take this one to table five over in the corner," her husband whispered in her ear. "Be careful around these guys."

She frowned. "Why?"

"Look at the way they wear their guns, like they're gunslingers. Right now, I don't trust them."

"Oh," she said suddenly glancing around at the men in the saloon, wondering if anyone else was a gunslinger.

A trickle of uneasiness gripped her and she understood the danger her husband dealt with on a daily basis. If he could do it, so could she.

Walking up to the table, she set the bottle down. "Hello, gentlemen, that will be twenty-five cents, please."

Another man leaned against the wall and stared at her. "Never seen you before."

"No," she said with a smile. "Lewis is my husband."

The man nodded and began to cough. Memories of her mother's influenza overwhelmed her causing her chest to ache with sadness. The illness started with a simple cough, but she refused to let Charity treat her.

"Are you all right?"

"A bit of a cold," he said, yet his complexion looked pale and didn't appear to be at his best.

With a frown, she told him, "Let me bring you some hot water and honey. Add your whiskey in with the honey and hot water, and in no time, you'll be better. It will soothe your throat and end the cough."

The gunslinger may be fast with his guns, but if he didn't drink the toddy and get rid of that cough, she feared for him. The cough started as nothing and slowly sapped her mother's strength, until that simple hacking noise left her lungs gurgling with fluid.

"How do you know this?"

Yet, her stubborn mother would not accept her help before it was too late. "My mother was a teetotaler. No liquor in the house. My grandmother made a mean toddy that would set you right in no time. All you boys could use a hot toddy if you've been out riding in the snow."

"Blizzard damn near killed us the other day," a man sitting at the table said, looking out from beneath his hat.

They all needed a little medical toddy to ward off the effects of the weather.

"Give me a moment and I'll bring you all the fixings for a hot toddy."

At the bar, Lewis glared at her, his frustration radiating from his eyes. "Didn't I tell you, not to linger at their table?"

The men were harmless, though she also recognized at any moment that could change, if they were provoked. Maybe she was naive, but a little goodwill never hurt anyone.

"The one man is ill and the others are not feeling well. The cough sounds like the start of influenza, at the very least, a cold. So I'm fixing some hot toddies for them and hopefully, they will soon be better."

Charity returned to their table and gave them the drinks. "What do we owe you for the drinks?"

"Nothing. Gentlemen, get better and come back to see us the next time you're in town."

She started to walk away when one of the men nearest her grabbed her hand. "Thank you, ma'am, but you forgot your tip."

Obviously, they were gunslingers. The men looked like someone who could become meaner than a rattlesnake in the hot sun if you crossed them. But they were still men and not feeling up to their best. As long as they didn't start a fight, she would welcome them like anyone else.

The man dropped two quarters in her hand.

"Thank you," she said quietly in awe of the money she had earned. In the last ten minutes, she made a whole fifty-five cents just by being friendly and helping her fellow human. Being a barmaid might be profitable and certainly not as bad as she thought.

Returning to the counter, she gazed at her husband. "Do you have a jar?"

"Well, yes," he said reaching onto a shelf beneath the bar. "What do you need it for?"

With a sigh, Charity put the coins into the jar. "These are my tips."

"What are you going to do with them?" he asked.

"Give them to Alice," she said. "She's a single mom, her son is sick, and she must not have anyone to care for him." Alice had a son to feed while Charity was doing fine. Biting her lip, she shook her head. "No, I don't need it. She does."

If the barmaid had been here tonight, this money would have been hers, not Charity's. Now, Charity overflowed with happiness at how her life went from escaping being a homeless person to a woman with a husband. And more wealth than she'd experienced in years.

Once you lost something, you perceived the value you'd squandered and come to expect.

For a moment, Lewis's mouth fell open and he sighed. "It's your decision."

Somewhere inside her, a flirtatious vixen awakened and she winked at her husband. "You're right. This is my decision. Now, what else do you have for me?"

This was fun and she enjoyed being around Lewis and working with him. For the first time, she felt a part of their business, like she shared in making their trade successful.

Laughing, he reached out and squeezed her arm. "There's a table in the corner that ordered some shots."

In a whirl, she turned from the bar, her skirts swished as she moved through the saloon to the table.

"Here you go, twenty cents, please," she said with a smile.

The man glared at her. "Where's Alice. Are you taking her job?"

The man was protective of the woman. All during the war, she learned to always pay attention to her gut reaction to someone. With this man, her gut screamed out warnings and she took a step back from the table.

"Not at all. Alice's son is sick and I'm filling in."

When she turned to walk away, the man grabbed her arm and pulled her into his lap. "Look at all that hair. What's your name, pretty girl?"

Stunned, Charity didn't know what to do until her Irish temper exploded and she reacted. The only available weapon was the tray holder and she slammed the wood against the man's head.

"Don't touch me," she shouted and threw a punch at him, hitting him on the cheekbone, her hand tingling. Out of the corner of her eyes, she saw her husband running. Lewis reached her side, and yanked her off the man's lap, his fist smashing into the man's face.

"That's my wife." With a vicious yank, Lewis hauled the limp man by the collar to the door where he tossed him into the street. "Don't come back. Nobody gets away with being disrespectful to my wife."

Lewis walked back in the saloon, he glanced around the room, his face a brilliant red, his breathing harsh. "Anyone else who grabs my wife will receive the same treatment."

With a firm grip on her elbow, he escorted her to the counter. "No one touches what's mine."

A sensation of warmth flooded her as she gazed at the man she married, her pulse racing. No one had ever defended her honor before. The act left her hungry to move her mouth over his in a kiss that would leave them both aching for more. But that had to wait.

~

WHEN THE MAN reached out and grabbed Charity's arm, Lewis hurtled himself over the counter, just as she took the serving tray to the man's head. Like the speed of lightning, his wife definitely had an Irish temper to go with all that beautiful auburn hair.

Hair that if he didn't get a chance to run his hands through soon, he would die.

Between the two of them, the man had been nearly unconscious, so he couldn't hit him again. Besides, he feared once he got started, he wouldn't stop. And that surprised him. Normally he was the cool head in a fight.

The vision of Charity hitting and punching the client lit a fire in him that had him ready to beat the man senseless. Why was he having such a strong reaction to this woman, his wife?

Even when the cadets at the military academy made fun of him, he learned to walk away and never look back. They weren't his friends and never would be, so why risk expulsion fighting with them. Over the years, he'd developed a very thick skin.

Staring at her across the room, Pete, one of his regulars, started laughing. "Lewis, in the months since you've owned this bar, I've never seen you react so strongly. I think you're smitten."

Was he?

"We've been married a week," he replied, not taking his eyes off Charity, watching to make certain no one else wanted to test his patience.

"With women, sometimes it just takes one glance," the man said. "Looks like your wife has wrapped her apron strings around your heart. It's called love."

He gave the man a glare he hoped would warn him not to tread where he didn't belong. "You ever been in love, Pete?"

"I'm married, ain't I?"

"Wouldn't know. Never met your wife and you spend all your time here. Appears to me, you might be in love with that whiskey bottle."

The man sighed. "Seven children later, the wife doesn't want an eighth one, so I come here."

The thought of so many little ones frightened Lewis. Sure he wanted children someday, but not seven.

Lewis stared at the man. "Seven children?"

"That's right. You better watch out. The way you're looking at your missus, the two of you will soon be expecting."

Fear scurried down Lewis spine. No, he wasn't ready for children. Their marriage might end in thirty days.

The image of his father came to mind and he quickly pushed it away. There were two sides to every story. But his father said his mother knew his situation and his mother swore she didn't know the man was married.

Either way, he was the product of their union and born in shame. Never would any of his children be called a bastard. Never.

Glancing into the crowd, he found Charity and she turned and smiled at him, reassuring him she was all right. At the sight of her full lips turned up, her emerald eyes twinkling with mischief, his heart pounded, his body calling out to hers like a siren.

Oh yeah, they were in danger of crossing the finish line in advance of thirty days.

Why did he feel like his life would never be the same? How long could he keep his true identity from her? How long could he keep his hands off his beautiful wife whose quick temper he would experience when she found out the truth?

"Yes, any day now, you're going to announce a baby arriving in eight months," Pete said, watching him.

A family of his own would be wonderful, but first he wanted the ownership of the saloon settled. No lingering secrets.

Then he would welcome Charity into his arms and his bed and anywhere else.

"Shut up and drink your whiskey, Pete."

The man laughed a knowing smirk on his lips.

CHARITY EARNED a whopping three dollars in tips and for the first time in a week, she felt productive. It was nice having someplace to go and work and earn money while she helped.

The next evening when she took Lewis his evening meal, she gazed around the saloon longingly. After last night, she wanted to work.

"Alice is back tonight," Lewis said, watching her.

"Why don't I help you? I'll be your second barmaid."

The idea of going back into that small apartment and staring at the four walls was enough to make her Irish temper start to awaken like a tiger waking from a nap.

"Don't need another one."

Why did she think he wasn't going to let her do anything? After last night's altercation with a drunk, he didn't want her here. But she must do something other than stare into space.

"Then let me tend bar. Let me serve drinks which would free you to do other things."

"No, I like tending bar."

With a frown, she glared at him, needing to somehow figure out how he was going to let her stay and work. The idea of returning upstairs was like being sentenced to a firing squad.

"Then what can I do?"

Already she could see the no forming on his lips as he shook his head and stared at her, his sapphires flashing with determination. The man was about to meet her stubborn streak, but she still had a few hidden tricks.

"After having to defend your honor last night, I think for your safety it would be best if you go back to the apartment."

She stared into his blue eyes and met a wall of resistance. Oh no, this was going to take some major womanly persuasion.

"Besides, I didn't think you liked the saloon. Wanted me to sell the business. Liquor is the devil's brew..."

Biting down on her bottom lip, she gave him her best flirtatious smile, tilting her head as she tried to put on a surprised look. "Believe me, I'm just as surprised as you are. How did I know that last night I would enjoy the work? Plus, I made three dollars."

Taking his hand, she rubbed her thumb over the top of his wrist and watched as his eyes widened. "Why can't we work together? If I help you, we'll have more time with one another."

Lewis's eyes flashed with confusion and she squeezed his hand and moved closer to him, going in for the kill. "After what happened, I know you're going to protect me. As long as you're here, watching over me, I'm not afraid."

Releasing his hand, she reached up and stroked the side of his face, using every feminine wile she'd ever learned.

A growl deep in his throat let her know she better stop. "Mrs. Huntington, you're very good at persuading me. The next time a man touches you in appropriately, you're back upstairs. Do you understand me?"

"Of course," she said, longing to throw her arms around him and kiss him, but knowing that would need to wait until later. Right now, she needed something to keep her busy. "Thank you. Much longer and I would've gone stir crazy."

Shaking his head, Lewis led her behind the bar. "Let me show you how to pour whiskey."

A buxom blonde woman wearing a low-cut blouse and a full skirt stepped up to the bar. "Table three needs three whiskeys."

"Alice, meet my wife, Charity. She's going to be working the saloon, helping me."

The woman gave her a quick once over and frowned. "Heard you two got married. Welcome to Angel Creek."

Excited to be introduced to his husband's employee and hoping for a new friend, Charity dug in her pocket. "Here, I collected this for you last night."

The barmaid reached out and took the change and shoved the money in her blouse. "Obliged. Now I need three whiskeys."

Shocked, Charity jumped when the woman snatched the money and then ignored her. After all, she could have kept the tips, but she wanted to help the single mother. Maybe she had a hard time accepting charity or maybe she was just rude.

Maybe the woman knew about the boy behind the saloon. "Did you see a young man about twelve to thirteen years of age near the back door," Charity asked.

"That's Isaac," the woman responded rolling her eyes. "Don't mind him. He's an orphan. Has no place to go."

Before Charity could respond, she turned and walked away. "Not very friendly, is she."

The woman acted angry that Charity would work with her in the saloon. The way she spoke of Isaac made Charity wonder what kind of mother would accept a child bedding down in the snow.

"She's working hard and her son is still ill. Do you want me to chase that boy away? Is he bothering you?"

Dismayed, Charity glanced at her husband, astounded he would even consider. "Not unless you want my fury unleashed on you. I'm worried about him. How can he continue to live outside in this weather?"

"Honey, you can't worry about every kid that lives on the street," he said. "We need to learn to take care of each other."

The thought of that poor boy out in the winter cold with no place to get warm left her feeling like a snapping turtle, wanting to bite the hand that fed her.

"Agreed, but when I gaze at him, it's my face I see. So easily that might have been me."

If she hadn't answered the ad in the Groom's Gazette, she would be living in a box on the street right now.

"You're here with me. Make sure the drinks are ready for Alice when she gets back from waiting on customers."

"Yes, but we're not through talking about Isaac," she said, tipping the whiskey bottle. Carefully, Charity measured out the alcohol. The drinks sat waiting while Alice seemed to deliberately stay away.

"Order up," Charity yelled out in the crowd.

When Alice came to the counter, she grabbed the three glasses and placed them on her tray and hurried away.

The next time she came to the bar, Charity was handling the drink orders by herself. Lewis disappeared into the back to bring up another barrel.

The barmaid slid behind the bar and whispered loud enough for Charity to hear over the noise. "Look, bitch, you may have married him, but he was my man long ago."

Astonished, Charity jerked back. "What do you mean?"

"I've had my eyes set on him since the day he moved into the saloon. My plans were to marry him."

There were so many ways Charity wanted to reciprocate. One included crawling over the bar, putting her arm around the woman's throat and manhandling her to the floor until she cried uncle.

The woman sparked a fire in her and one more comment would find the two of them head to head. To calm herself, she took a deep breath, and smiled, tossed her auburn hair back and leaned close to make certain the woman had no questions about her message. The smile was to lure the bitch to bait.

"First off, don't call the wife of the owner a bitch. That language could be detrimental to your job status. Second, we're married, so back away from *my* husband."

Gritting her teeth, she said loudly in her ear. "Third, we're going to get along. Now, let's pretend this conversation never took place. My husband thinks a lot of you, but I don't think marriage to you was on his mind. Time to get back to work. And smile when you talk to the patrons and me."

The woman gave her a snarky grin before she walked away. Now Charity wished she had kept the money and given it to the boy staying behind the bar. What was done could not be undone. Yet, maybe her son would benefit from their generosity.

A man sat on a bar stool in front of her. "What are you drinking?"

The big, burly man's eyes were cold and yet he gave her a smile that appeared forced. "You, sugar. I'd like a sip of you."

With a sideways glance, Charity looked around, her stomach tightening. Her husband wouldn't stand for any more trouble or she would find herself trapped in that small apartment. "Not possible, as I'm a happily married woman."

The man smiled. "Then I have a message for you from Mr. John Roberts III."

With a gulp, she stared at the rugged man. What did that despicable man want with her now?

LEWIS STEPPED out of the storeroom carrying a carton of whiskey and set it on the floor. As he stood in the doorway, he took a moment to catch his breath. Automatically, his eyes searched and found Charity at the bar, her face tense, her tone cold as she talked to a man in front of her. Something must have gone wrong.

Funny, in the short time they knew each other, he could read her facial expressions. His happy girl, the one who threw her head back and giggled, disappeared and in her place, a woman who looked like if she had a gun, the man would be staring up at the sky, sightless, right now.

Carrying the carton to the counter, she glanced at him, relief etched on her face. He heard the man say. "I'm not giving up."

She handed him a drink. "Enjoy."

The noise in the saloon was at a fever pitch as the hour became late and several of the men consumed quite a bit of liquor.

When he reached his wife, she whirled to face him. "There you are. I think I'm going to take a little break."

With that announcement, she headed for the door. Why did it appear as if she were escaping? What did the man say to her? Lewis almost flat out asked him, as the man was still there, but didn't want to upset Charity.

The man tossed back his drink, swallowing it in one gulp, slammed the glass down, stood and walked out the door. An uneasiness overcame Lewis and the urge to follow him was strong, but he had a saloon to run.

Alice strolled up to his side and laid her hand on his arm. "Your wife got caught talking to that man. Honey, I'm worried about you. Anytime you need to talk to someone, I'm always here for you."

Thank goodness, the counter stood between them as she leaned over and gave him an eyeful of her abundant breasts spilling out of her blouse. The move was meant to entice him, but it did the exact opposite. If only the woman realized his mother wore a similar type of dress. One intended to seduce a man, even a married man.

With disgust, Lewis stared at the woman. Sure, she flirted with him in the past, but he'd never given her any encouragement. While he had done all he could to help her, as a single mother, he held no interest. Too much of her situation reminded him of his mother and sent him running the other direction.

"Thanks, but I'm married."

With determination, Lewis moved down the bar away from Alice to the next customer signaling for a refill. Being married had been more fulfilling than he expected, but also trying. Trying because sleeping beside his Irish rebel, he woke with a hard on and went to bed with a hard on.

The best part of the day was waking curled around Charity, but watching other men gaze at her kept him ever watchful.

The friendliness of his wife with the patrons had increased his sales the last two nights, but he wasn't certain the worry made her presence worthwhile.

The man walked toward the door, leaving Lewis wondering who he was that caused such a distraught expression on his wife's face. Did she know him?

CHAPTER 6

*T*he winter sun shining brightly through the windows, three of the women gathered in Sarah's living room. Her home was the closest to all of them and they were spending the morning drinking coffee and catching up. Ruby was absent as she and her husband had been called out to fight a breakout of ague at the fort. Julia lived so far out of town, the drive was too dangerous in the snow.

As Charity glanced around the room at her friends, she sighed. "Lord o'mercy, I've missed you guys," she said walking into the room, hugging each one as she came inside. "How's married life?"

"I'm learning to cook," Sarah said with a sigh.

Anna laughed. "Levi doesn't know I drove the sleigh into town. I needed to see you. He goes out in the barn and works and works and being by myself gets boring. What about you, Charity?"

"Lewis is allowing me to work in the saloon," she said grinning.

The two friends gasped, their eyes turning toward her with shock and disbelief.

SYLVIA MCDANIEL

"Your mother..." Anna said. "Your family never drank."

"Yes, she would have been mortified, but I'm loving the chance to work. All the money I make in tips is mine to keep."

After doing without for so long, it felt wonderful to have money in her pocket. Not that Lewis had not been generous, but this money she earned on her own. In fact, she found a hiding place inside a book to squirrel away her cash.

She gazed at her friends' faces and realized they thought her job scandalous, but she didn't care. For once, she had some control. Like she wasn't sitting around darning socks for soldiers or making a wedding quilt she would never use.

For once, she was earning money and she planned on saving as much as possible in case of an emergency.

But there was her problem...one little hiccup that could ruin her plans.

"Do any of you know Mike Devillin?"

"Why?" Sarah asked, her face going pale.

"Last night, he showed up at the saloon. Told me John Roberts says I owe him a lot of money," she said, sighing.

"The name sounds familiar. Why?" Anna asked. "Why would he think you owe him money?"

"Mr. Devillin is known for doing dirty deeds for people in Charleston. Before we left, I lived in fear my in-laws would hire him to kill me," Sarah said.

"What's he doing here?" Anna asked.

"Uh, me," Charity said, knowing in her heart why Mr. Roberts sent his thug searching for her.

Charity understood she should be ashamed of the destruction, but somehow the man deserved the damage she created. Until now, she had not told her friends of her naughtiness.

"Because I redecorated the inside of the house before I left town. Now the house needs a make-over," she said.

"Oh, Charity, why would you do that?" Anna said with a groan.

Charity's blood started to simmer all over again. "That jerk is going to make my family home into a brothel. A whorehouse."

"Shhh, keep your voice down," Sarah said. "Becca is playing in her room, and I don't want her to hear such words."

Oops, Sarah was right to protect her daughter. Becca was a little young to learn about the oldest profession in the world at this time in her life.

"Sorry, but he wanted me to stay and work for him. Very generously, he would allow me to continue to live in my home as long as I worked exclusively for him."

The women's mouths dropped and stared at her in astonishment. While they were in Charleston, she kept this a secret, telling her friends nothing about how this man threatened, coerced, cajoled, did everything he could to convince her to become one of his girls. There was no way she would sleep with unknown men. Not even for her childhood home.

So she left him the shell of a house. The inside...needed work.

"John Roberts is lucky I didn't burn the thing down."

The old home held so many memories, she considered torching it, but knew that would get her in all kinds of trouble.

"Charity! What are you going to do?" Anna asked.

That question she kept asking herself over and over. How did one keep something like this from her husband? "Haven't decided. Still thinking."

"Maybe you should talk to Quinn," Sarah said, rising and going around and filling everyone's coffee cups. "Surely he could help you."

"Look, I did it, Sarah. I destroyed the walls of the house, so that the pimp would need to remodel the home. Quinn might arrest me," she said. The last night in the house, all the anger at what was to happen to her beloved home exploded with the help of a hammer.

"Every room?" Sarah asked.

"No, mainly the kitchen, the main room, and the bedrooms," she said remembering how hard it had been to smash the walls in her parents' bedroom.

Yet, she was certain they would have been pleased she made the pompous ladies' man pay more to repair their home. The very concept of what was going on inside the house spiraled a shiver of revulsion through her.

"Charity, you find more trouble," Anna reprimanded.

With a shrug of her shoulders, she nodded. What could she say, it was true. Her mother always told her that her father's Irish temper passed on to her.

"Not on purpose. Mr. Devillin approached me after our pesky barmaid told me I stole her man, my husband. What am I going to do?"

Anna started laughing. "Wait, I'm confused. What are you going to do about what? The barmaid or Mr. Devillin?"

"Both," Charity said, starting to grow irritated at Anna.

The woman was like milk toast, with little or no backbone.

"Alice will be seeing stars and on the next stagecoach out of town if she messes with Lewis. If Mr. Devillin thinks I'm going to repay Mr. Roberts so he can build his brothel, he'll be waiting for the south to rise again. I'd rather spend time in jail than give money to that man."

"It's no longer your home," Sarah said softly. "Your place is here now."

That was true, but the dilemma followed her all the way to Montana and she doubted he would leave without a fight. Now she wanted him gone for good. And Alice may be a single mother, but the woman had a nasty streak like a pole cat, that ran down her spine.

"My life seems so simple compared to yours. Washing, cooking, washing, repeat. Okay, my life in the woods is looking better by the second. I'll stay with my Levi," Anna said. "But how are we going to help you?"

All last night, Charity tossed and turned trying to decide what her plan of action should be. If she told Lewis, she feared his reaction. If she didn't tell Lewis, could this man make her go with him? Also, she worried if keeping a secret from her husband was the best thing for her marriage.

"Don't know. This is not something I want to tell Lewis. He's so protective of me, I'm afraid of what he would do to the man. Yet, I don't think it's fair to keep this from him."

"Do you like Lewis?" Anna asked.

Sarah giggled. "What do you mean, does she like him? They're sleeping together."

"Hey, don't tell Anna all my secrets."

"Well, for now at least they're only *sleeping* together," Sarah said with a laugh.

Anna stared at Charity. "Are you ready to have sex with your husband?"

Charity gave it some thought. Her handsome husband, the way he watched over her and cared for her, the way he made sure she always had what she needed. His kisses, his thoughtfulness. The idea was both frightening, and exciting. For over a week, she'd been questioning herself, but suddenly no more.

"Oh yes, I'm ready to make our marriage a real one. But first, I have to deal with the pimp's collector."

A COUPLE DAYS later while Lewis prepared for the evening rush, a man walked into the saloon and up to the counter, his boots echoing on the wooden floor. "Letter for Jakob Huntington."

Lewis ignored the man until he remembered he was Jakob. "That's me."

He handed him the envelope and Lewis reached inside his pocket and pulled out change for a tip. Charity had gone upstairs to prepare their dinner that she probably would burn. His wife quickly learned how to tend bar and connect with the clients, but cooking, she still needed some instruction.

For a rich, southern belle, adjusting to a new life, she was doing well.

Glancing at the envelope, he stared at the name as worry slinked up the length of his spine. With a deep breath, he took out his knife, ripped the envelop open and quickly read the missive.

Dear Son,

Hope this letter finds you well and business in the saloon bustling. From the reports I've received, the business is doing well and the accounts are being paid on time. I'm so proud of how you finally settled down and became responsible.

Yes, I realize finding you a wife was none of my business, but I couldn't resist playing matchmaker. My sources told me you married and you're enjoying the mail-order bride I sent you and the two of you are happy. It seemed like a good idea at the time, but I'm sure a woman arriving must have been quite a surprise.

Sometime soon I'm going to come visit you. Before that time, I'm hoping you'll write and tell me that a grandchild is on the way.

When you're a father, you'll understand why I took the actions I did to make you into a better man. A man who takes his responsibilities serious.

Until then.

Your Father.

Lewis cursed beneath his breath. Walking into the office, he laid the missive on his desk and considered responding to the man's correspondence. All he needed was a little more time before he would be able to purchase the saloon.

In the meantime, who in town watched over him and reported back to Mr. Huntington? Could it be Charity or someone else who let the man know his every move? Obviously, the spy didn't know he was not Jakob. That man was dead.

Sitting at the desk, he sighed. Before Charity came downstairs and saw the letter, he had to file it away. If he replied, he feared his handwriting would give him away and the man would comprehend he wasn't Jakob. So instead, he locked the correspondence away, praying Mr. Huntington wouldn't arrive until spring.

Hopefully, the last blizzard closed the trails and he had time before the man arrived on his doorstep.

While Lewis loved owning his own business, he doubted his decision about taking Jakob Huntington up on his offer. Yet if he hadn't taken the chance, he would never have met the most stunning, beautiful, woman, his wife. Someone who would never consider him before. Someone he hoped would never leave him when the truth was revealed.

The correspondence from Jakob's father made him question his own. Could his father still be searching for him?

If Mr. Huntington showed up in town, he would easily locate the saloon, but how would the man react to the knowledge his son was dead. How would his father react when he learned his location?

THE NEXT DAY, close to closing time, Charity carried a dish pan full of dirty water to the back door. When she opened the door, the boy jumped back, just as she tossed the water, barely missing the kid.

"Oh, I'm so sorry," she called as he slid down the wall away from her. "Wait? Are you hungry? I've got some leftover stew if you'd like a bowl."

"Don't take no handouts," he said, continuing to move away from her.

The boy had pride, but what could she have him do to give him some food? "There is something you could help me with. My husband only handles our trash about once a week and with the saloon, we need someone to start the fire more often. How about I give you food every day and you burn our garbage for us?"

She watched him in the shadows, contemplating his options. "What's your name, boy?"

"Isaac, ma'am."

"That's a biblical name."

Where were the boy's parents? His family? The people who once cared for him. How unlucky to grow up living in poverty on the streets alone.

"Yes, ma'am."

"So do you want the job or not?"

"Can I have a bowl of that stew right now? Then I'll get started on your trash."

The kid must be starving. Maybe Lewis would hire him full time and they could give him room and board as well. Anything to get this child into a safe warm place to stay.

"Sure," she said. "Give me a moment."

In fewer than five minutes, she returned with a steaming bowl of beef stew and handed it to the boy along with a piece of cornbread. In Charleston, many nights she went without eating, but watching this child almost inhale the food, brought back all those terrible memories.

All the times her stomach gnawed empty and hurting and longing for something to eat. The loneliness after everyone died. The fear some man would think she was an easy target.

And yet here was Isaac living the same life only without shelter from the cold, struggling to survive. Just like she would have been if she had not left Charleston. Isaac returned the empty bowl and pointed to the piles of empty containers. "You want all this burned?"

"Yes, please," she said. "Sleep closer to the fire."

"Thank you, miss," he said. "Thank you."

The boy bundled up the garbage and put it in a barrel. In a

moment, he struck a match and lit a flame. The fire illuminated where he'd been sleeping.

Against the building, he had piled up the snow to make a barrier from the wind. An old tattered blanket lay on top of some boards where the kid slept. The temperature was falling and she hoped the blaze would keep him warm.

"Place a brick or a rock in the fire and then put it inside your blanket. The warmth from the brick will keep you toasty."

Another fact she learned during those frigid winter nights when she had little wood to keep the fire burning.

"Tomorrow evening I'll bring you food and you will take care of the trash," she said. "This will be a big help for my husband."

How the boy had survived this long, she didn't know. But someone needed to help this child. And that person would be her.

The door behind her opened and the boy darted back into inky darkness, hiding.

"What are you doing?" Lewis asked. "Did you set the garbage on fire? I told you I would do it."

Glancing around, she didn't want Lewis to frighten Isaac. "Yes, I started it. Now come back inside out of this cold."

He gazed at her strangely and glanced down at the dish in her hand. Together they went back to the bar and she wondered if she should be honest and tell him about Isaac.

"Occasionally, we all need a little help in life."

"Be careful. Not everyone can be trusted."

Why did people think a child on the streets was suspicious? In that moment, her Irish temper flared at the unfairness of life. It wasn't the boy she didn't trust. Rather the men in her life who had gone off to war and left her destitute and now facing a problem of her own creation.

Maybe she was the one that shouldn't be trusted. After all, she was keeping a secret from her husband.

"What about you, Lewis? Can you be trusted?"

What made her ask the question, she didn't know. Sometimes her husband got this far away look in his eyes and he never mentioned his family. What secrets was Lewis concealing? Were they anything like hers?

CHAPTER 7

*O*n Sunday morning, Lewis forced himself to crawl out of bed. If he stayed beside his wife any longer, he feared their thirty-day waiting period would end right then. Waking beside his wife each morning, grew harder and harder. The urge to curl around her and wrap her in his embrace had him yanking back the covers and stumbling out of bed.

Quietly, he made his way into the kitchen where he pulled out his bookkeeping. The plan was to finish before Charity woke. Not that he didn't trust her, but he couldn't concentrate when she was around, and for once in his life, he wanted to be a success.

For the next twenty minutes, he balanced the books, so he could order his next supply of liquor. Eventually after he owned Angel Creek Palace, he wanted to put in a small kitchen. Maybe if the men who came in ate a little something along with their drink, they wouldn't stagger out the door.

"What are you doing?" she asked.

Married fewer than two weeks, already they'd fallen into a routine. One that so far, he enjoyed. Lazy mornings together and then they went to work in the saloon. While he stocked the shelves, she made sure the glasses were clean and everything sparkled, ready to go for the evening.

"The bookwork. On Sunday, I like to record the receipts, pay the bills and compare our revenue and expenses."

"Are we doing all right?" Anxiety trembled in her voice, panic radiating in her gaze.

Losing everyone in the war left his wife determined not to be broke again. Not that she was greedy. Oh no, she was one of the most sharing, caring individuals he ever had the privilege to help. But fear lingered in her eyes at the mention of money.

Food was something she never wanted to run out of and purchased daily at the mercantile.

Losing everything, she tried to help those less fortunate, by feeding the boy out back. Probably the very reason she worked beside him at night, not only to be with him, but also to make the extra cash in tips.

Being penniless left a person vulnerable and neither of them wanted to experience that situation again.

To ease her concerns, he smiled at her, knowing as long as Mr. Huntington didn't come to town they were safe. "We're doing great. In fact, since my wife has gone to work in the saloon, our profits have almost doubled. People like you."

With a sigh of relief, she sank down in a chair across from him. She reached out and touched his hand, sending his heart palpitating. The woman had no clue as to the effect she had on him and probably half the men in his saloon.

The time she served in the bar, he worried about her, yet she seemed to enjoy being around people and sitting up in the apartment left her frustrated. Since she started working beside him, she seemed happier.

Charity needed to be around people.

"All I do is talk to them. Ask about their wives and kids and they tell me their life story. How the war affected them. It's odd how they disclose the most personal details," she said squeezing his hand.

"What do you say back to them?"

"Honestly?" she said with a laugh. "Last night I told Frank if he wanted his marriage to work, maybe he should consider going home to his wife instead of hanging out at our bar. And he did."

"That's not good for profits," Lewis teased, not really upset by her actions. The man needed to go home and be with his family.

"No, but there seems to be two kinds of people who come in. Lonely cowboys and lonely married men."

The cowboys he worried the least about since normally they only had time to come in on weekends. The married men in town were either unhappy or trying to escape for the evening. Or like Pete, didn't want to make their women pregnant again. After all, once the kids went down, there was just the two of you.

Lewis wanted children, he wanted a family of his own, eventually.

A smart woman, Charity knew their clientele.

"You left out the men who just want to get drunk and aren't allowed alcohol at home," he said wanting to lean over and kiss his wife. With a toss of her red curls, the need to pull her mouth to his overwhelmed him, but he resisted.

"Those are the regulars. The men you see there every night and I don't like them very well," she said. "What would you like for breakfast? We should have made it to church this morning."

They needed to stay involved in the community and going to a service on Sunday was one way to do that. Yet he felt like such a hypocrite among religious people. The bastard child of a military man who had an affair with his mother and now ran a saloon. Why would those people want to be around him?

"Were your parents religious?" she asked.

What should he tell her about his father? The way the pompous man never had time for him as a child. At least, not until Lewis was old enough to enter military school where he was ridiculed.

Was he ready to let her know she married a man shunned by polite society? Once he'd been engaged to a beautiful young woman he met at a cotillion. When she learned of his background, she called off the wedding and dumped him publicly.

"My mother was Catholic, my father..." He didn't know what religion his father was except for the United States Military—the only doctrine General Scott followed and expected his son, all of them, to follow, including Lewis. Only he rebelled.

"No, my family wasn't religious," he said, thinking they had never attended church together. Never. "What about you?"

"Oh yes, we went every Sunday. What about our children?" she asked.

"Are you expecting?"

"Yes, immaculate conception," she said, flirting with him.

A grin spread across his face. Why did the idea of having children with her fill him with warmth and a sense of homecoming? Would she accept he was illegitimate and learn to love him and all his faults? Or would she be like JoAnn the debutante, who said she could never marry below her?

This was becoming so real. Every day that passed brought them closer together. Soon thirty days would end, and well, he didn't want to lose her, but she didn't know the truth. Would she forgive him for lying and being a bastard?

"We'll make that decision when we need to, but I'm sure we'll attend church as a family."

No way would his children ever suffer what he went through. No way would they be ostracized. Their father would be present in their lives, giving them guidance and never abandoning their mother.

He watched her stand and walk to his side of the table. Uncertain as to her intent, he almost groaned as she leaned down and brushed her lips across his. Unable to resist, he pulled her into his lap.

The feel of her soft derriere against him was enough to make him groan. How lucky could a man be? Placing his hands on her cheeks, he held her in place as his mouth ravaged hers. It was the like the kiss a man gave his lover. A kiss designed to ignite passion.

When he released her, her breathing was harsh, her lips swollen and her eyes glossy, veiled by her red-tipped lashes. Inside, he felt giddy that his wife was affected by his kisses. Suddenly, she stood and took him by the hand, pulling him to his feet, his heart beating erratically in his chest.

"Where are we going?" he asked. Right now, there was only one place he wanted to go with her.

"Back to bed," she said, gazing at him her eyes glazed with desire that he created.

Happiness had him crushing her against his chest, her soft breasts tightly against him as he moaned deep in his throat. "We can't unless..."

"Yes," she whispered. "Unless you have objections."

"Oh, hell no."

Not wanting to stop, Lewis swept Charity up in his arms and carried her into their bedroom and kicked the door closed. No matter what happened in the future, she would always be his wife.

LATER IN THE AFTERNOON, they lay in bed in each other's arms.

"Now I truly feel like a married woman," she said, gazing into her husband's sapphire eyes that looked like a cloudless sky. The only thing that could have made this morning more perfect was if Lewis confessed his love for her.

Still, they were getting to know one another. She had no doubts sooner or later, one of them would say those three words that meant so much to her.

They signaled commitment, attachment, and the willingness to stay together through thick and thin and everything in between. Like icing on a cake, those three words were sweet and delicious. Oh, how she wanted this precious moment between the two of them to last forever without the world intruding.

Though their thirty days was not up, she was certain she would remain married to Lewis. No way she would end their relationship after sleeping in the same bed, after laughing and giggling and loving her time with her husband.

Fewer than two weeks ago, she walked into this small apartment and wondered what she had done. Now she knew. She found a man worthy of spending her life with.

At night in the saloon, she watched him turn away men who consumed too much whiskey and give a hungry man a handout. Then there was the barmaid, Alice. After Charity witnessed Lewis turning away that siren's advances, she no longer worried about him cheating. If the woman recognized his look of disgust, she wouldn't try again.

While he tried to hide his emotions, inside this man a strong, clear mind strove to do good and what more could you want in a hardworking man? Her father always told her he'd take a soldier with a conscious and good set of morals over any man who joined the army for food and board any day.

In some ways, Lewis reminded her of her father and that couldn't be bad.

"You are a married woman," he said, his hand trailing down her naked back. "For better or worse, richer or poorer."

"In sickness and in health," she said.

"Until death do us part," he replied as his mouth covered hers.

With a sigh, she let his tongue tease her until once again she was eager for his touch.

This Sunday would be the day she would always remember as the day they consummated their marriage and began their life together. This day, she realized, she was falling in love with her husband and wanted a family, a life with this man.

This day, all her dreams were coming true.

LEWIS SAT across from his wife and stared at the beautiful woman. He'd yet to tell her she was married to a bastard. From talking to her, he understood she came from a wealthy background and he wondered if she would react like his fiancée.

Today, they consummated their marriage. While having sex brought them closer than they'd ever been, he feared her reaction about him not only being illegitimate, but lying to her *and* impersonating someone else. Would she still accept him as her husband or would she leave?

Though he didn't want to admit it to himself, he was starting to fall in love with this beautiful woman. The sound of her laughter, the way she treated everyone the same in his saloon. The interaction with his clientele. Her benevolent nature in helping the homeless young man who lived behind them.

All those things warmed his heart and he hoped she would be as forgiving and generous with him as she was with the people she met.

How could something that seemed like such a great idea at the time, a chance at a new start, have turned out to be so bad? How he wanted to be completely honest with her, but not yet. When he purchased the saloon, he would tell her everything. And then what?

"Would you do me a favor?" she asked.

"Anything," he said, thinking right now if she asked for a mountain of gold, he would move heaven and earth to find it for her.

"Would you employ Isaac to work in the saloon? I've been giving him food for burning our garbage, but the boy should have a place to shelter at night. A chance at an education."

Hiring Isaac was the one thing he didn't feel comfortable doing. On several occasions, he helped the boy, but he didn't want to hire him out right because the kid didn't look a day over thirteen.

The boy didn't need to be around liquor or drunks. Yet, the kid probably had seen far worse. Plus, that was more money out of his pocket instead of going toward purchasing the saloon.

"He's a good kid who's had a poor start in life," she said.

"How do you know," he asked.

With a tilt of her head, her red curls spilled from her shoulder and the urge to reach out and pull her into his arms once again overwhelmed him. As he trailed his fingers across the soft, silky skin of her naked shoulder, he realized he couldn't get enough of her.

"I don't," she said. "Something about him says he needs our help. And I want to do what I can for him."

Lewis sighed and wanted to tell her out right no, but he couldn't do that. It would crush her and today, of all days, he wanted to make his bride happy.

"The reason I haven't hired him in the past is because I don't want a young man of his age working in my saloon. He doesn't need to be influenced by alcohol. Though, I understand work would be such a help. I'll promise you this, I'll talk to some of the men in town and see if I can find him a job doing something."

Hopefully, it was a compromise they both would be able to live with.

A smile crossed her face. "Thank you. The boy wants to

work. Told me he wouldn't take handouts. That's why I let him burn our trash. Besides, it gives you more time to spend with me."

Never in his life could Lewis remember feeling this happy. "My wife is a very smart person who knows how to obtain what she wants. I need to remember this."

The woman could twist him around her and he would do anything to make her happy. And when she learned of her power, he would be doomed. His wife was smart, beautiful, and had crawled inside his heart and taken control. There was nothing he wouldn't do for her.

"Now about that bookwork you started on this morning. Do you need some help?" she asked.

If she grasped how much he hated keeping track of the expenses and the revenue, she wouldn't have to ask. "After dinner, we can work on it together. Maybe you can help me balance everything and we can make a simpler system of doing the bookwork."

"I'd love to help you," she said. "But there's a charge for my help."

"What's that?"

Confusion spiraled through him as he stared at her. What would she need?

"We come back to bed afterward," she said smiling.

"Oh my, didn't you get enough, woman?" he said, grinning, loving the way they were together.

A grin spread across her face as she tossed her curly red hair off her shoulders. "No."

An emotion never experienced before rocked him and he wanted this moment to always be like this between them. Fear filled him.

THE NEXT DAY, Charity was so tempted to run to Sarah's house and tell her all about what had gone on between her and Lewis. Right now, she wanted to savor the moments and keep this little tidbit of information to herself.

The time she spent in Lewis's arms had been the most precious time she could recall in her life. And she prayed their life together only became stronger.

One settling secret remained between them. The appearance of Mr. Devillin. She almost told Lewis about the hated man but decided their special day should not be marred by talk of problems. Sooner or later, she knew she would have to confess and tell him the man wanted her back in Charleston.

Though she missed her home, she would never go back. Maybe she should talk to Quinn, Julia's husband. Dismay filled her at the idea of him locking her in jail for what she'd done.

Tonight, once again, she worked in the saloon and hoped the dreaded man didn't show up and force her to tell her husband. As she finished serving clients, she hurried back to the bar. Alice gave her a once over and when Lewis walked away, she turned to Charity.

"Isaac asked me to give you a message. Said he needed to talk to you right away. He's waiting for you in the back."

The way she said *Isaac* let Charity know right away what she thought of the boy. "Is he hurt?"

"Didn't say. Just said you needed to come out as soon as possible. I'll handle serving while you go check on him."

For a moment, Charity considered telling Lewis, but he was busy pouring drinks at the other end of the counter. Instead, she rushed out the side door that would take her into the back where the spare liquor was stored.

When she opened the door, she stared into the darkness. An eerie feeling came over her at the silence. "Isaac, are you here?"

No response. If the boy wanted to speak with her, where was he? She stepped outside. "Isaac?"

A hand came over her mouth and she struggled against the arm that coiled around her chest, pulling her snug against him. Fear exploded inside her and she tried to scream. "Shut up. I'm taking you back to Charleston."

Never in a hundred years would she return to her hometown. Her home was here with her husband.

Lifting her elbow, she tried to punch him, but he was too strong and held her in a firm grip. He shoved a rag into her mouth and secured it around her head, keeping her from screaming. Next, he wrapped her arms in front of her with rope before he guided her out of the alley.

In the inky gloom, she heard a scurrying noise and looked to see Isaac hiding. With a jerk of her head, she tried to tell him to get Lewis, but didn't know if he understood her.

The cold seeped into her bones and she shivered as he dragged her to two horses. Like a bag, he tossed her across the first one and she tried to spur the animal with her feet. The man was quick, grabbing the bit and controlling the horse.

With a chuckle, he helped her sit up and then tied the reins of her horse to his own saddle. "Now we'll ride all the way to Denver and catch the train from there."

Glancing back at the saloon, pain ripped her chest at leaving Lewis. Now her home was here with her husband and she didn't want to go back to Charleston. She refused to work in a brothel for any man. But John Roberts was a prominent citizen. Would anyone believe her story?

CHAPTER 8

*L*ewis glanced around the saloon. Where was Charity? In the last fifteen minutes, he hadn't seen her and that made him nervous.

Alice stepped up to the bar. "Four whiskeys for the table in the corner."

"Have you seen Charity?"

"Nope, I've been busy covering for her. You know the next time you want to think about bringing a woman in, you should talk to me first."

When he hired Alice, it was because he thought as a single mother, she needed help. But sometimes she overstepped her bounds. After he told everyone he and Charity were married, she continued to press up against him.

He had no interest in Alice before he married Charity. Even now, too many things about her reminded him of his past life. And he refused to cheat on his wife. The result of the general and his mother cheating years ago, he vowed never to bring on his family the shame he carried.

As far as he was concerned, his wife had nothing to fear from him with regard to infidelity. There were consequences to your actions and he often wondered if the general ever confessed to his wife he had another son.

If Alice didn't stop, she would soon find herself looking for another job. After he poured the whiskeys, she whisked the drinks to a table. Out of the corner of his eye, he saw Isaac standing at the back door in his tattered clothes. The boy really did need some help.

Alice rushed over and scolded the boy. He couldn't hear what she said to him, but she tried to shove the kid out the door, pushing him back.

Something in the boy's face alarmed him. She slapped the kid and he'd seen enough. Jumping over the counter, he ran to the boy. Why would she hit the kid unless she wanted to keep the kid from Lewis?

"What's wrong," Lewis said, racing to Isaac's side.

"Mr. Huntington," he screamed. "Hurry. That man took your wife. He's getting away."

The words sent a chill spiraling down Lewis's spine. His chest clenched with pain as fury begin to burn inside him. The boy wasn't lying. "What man?"

"The man who rode into town this week, searching for Miss Kingston."

Charity's maiden name. The man must know her and for some reason came to kidnap her. Could it be the same man who spoke to her two days ago and left the distressed expression on her face?

"Go to the sheriff and tell him what's happened. Gentlemen, we're officially closed."

Frank stood. "Did you say someone took Mrs. Charity, your wife?"

"Yes, I'm heading out after her now."

"Come on, boys, we need to help this man find his wife. Then we're going to kick the scalawag's ass clean out of the state."

Stunned at the outpouring of help, Lewis grabbed his coat. Before he could leave, he would need to get his horse at the stable. In front of him, about ten men ran out of the saloon to go after his wife.

Anxious, he hurried out the door.

"Take my horse, Lewis, it will be faster," Pete, one of his regulars, said.

"Thank you, much obliged."

Lewis had no idea which way to ride in the snow, but then he found the tracks. In the darkness, the man couldn't be far.

Nobody took what was his. And Charity was his wife.

CHARITY HUNG on to the saddle horn, shivering in the cold. The man hadn't given her a coat or let her grab hers as they rode through the snow. He told her she'd soon be warm enough and she had a terrible suspicion about what she would experience when they stopped.

Her Irish temper was fully engaged and ready to fight to the death before the man touched her again.

She did her best to slow her horse, but Mr. Devillin held the reins and she hung on as they galloped crazily in the night. After they left, she hoped Isaac rushed inside and told Lewis. At this moment, she prayed Lewis was on his way to rescue her.

It was her only chance. No way would she ever work in a whorehouse.

Suddenly he pulled their horses off the trail and into some brush. In a mad dash, he picked up a tree branch, and concealed their tracks. When he came back, he gave her a threatening look.

"Keep quiet or your husband is dead."

The thought of Lewis being killed frightened her. How

could she live with herself if he died because of her stupidity? Maybe provoking a powerful brothel owner by tearing up the inside of her home was not the smartest thing she might have done. Yet, what he planned for the house left her sick. No way she would make it easy for him.

In the darkness, the sound of horses racing toward them had her squirming, needing to scream, but with a rag in her mouth, there was nothing she could do. Not even whistle Dixie.

Without the reins, she couldn't control the animal. But she could pinch him. Cringing inside as she didn't want to hurt the horse, but maybe he would make some noise. Something to alert her husband she was here and he was about to ride past her.

With a sigh, she took her fingernail and dug into the poor animal's side, guilt making her squirm. If this worked, she would personally give the horse an extra bag of oats. The animal squealed and danced around trying to get away from the pain and she felt bad for hurting it.

Mr. Devillin glared at her and walked over to check out why the animal cried out.

"Stop," she heard Lewis shout.

The burly man pulled out his Colt and waved it at her, pointing the gun at her heart. Evil radiated from his gaze, his shining eyes letting her know he wouldn't hesitate to kill her.

"Did anyone else hear anything?"

The riders came to a halt and they waited. She wanted to shout, but fear of a bullet slamming into her chest kept her silent. Now was not the time for her to die. There was so much life left to live with the man she was falling in love with.

"Let's go," Lewis said loudly and her head fell to her chest, dejected. They were moving on. A tear trickled down her cheek at the sound of horses galloping away.

The man smiled at her, confident the search party had gone on as he slipped his Colt back into the holster. Sadness overwhelmed her at the thought of her husband thinking she left on her own.

In the shadow of the moonlight, through the trees, she saw a shadowy figure, moving stealthily and recognized Lewis. Freezing her emotions, she kept a sad mask on her face while her heart raced at the sight of her husband sneaking up on the man.

The man jumped at the feel of a gun shoved in his back. "Nobody takes what's mine."

"The bitch owes my creditor money."

"That doesn't give you the right to kidnap her."

Charity had never seen such a murderous expression on Lewis's face. For a moment, she feared he was going to shoot the man as he jabbed the pistol in his back multiple times, causing the man to flinch.

"I'd like nothing better than to shoot you," Lewis said. "But I won't.

Gripping the man by the shirt, he poked the gun in the man's neck. "We're going back to the sheriff's office and discuss this matter. Charges will be filed. If the boys from the saloon find you, you'll leave town in a box. My wife has quite a following at the saloon and they didn't appreciate you taking their favorite waitress."

Warmth shivered through her veins that the men in the saloon helped search for her. The danger of frostbite left her shaking in the cold air. The men must be somewhere close. The feeling in her fingers was gone and if she didn't have a blanket or jacket or something soon, she would have frostbite.

The sheriff rode into the bushes where they were hiding. "What's going on here?"

"This man kidnapped my wife."

"I was taking her back to pay her debts."

Charity moaned hoping to draw Lewis's attention. She wanted the cloth out of her mouth, so she could viscerate this man with her tongue. When she got through with him, he would never have relations with a woman ever again.

Quinn glanced at Charity. "Usually when a woman's mouth is covered and her hands are all tied up, it's not because she's going back willingly. Now, we need to have a frank discussion about the penalties for kidnapping."

The sheriff climbed off his horse and slapped handcuffs on the man's wrists. "Let's go back to the jail where we can sit down and review what's going on."

Once Quinn had Mr. Devillin in custody, Lewis ran to Charity and helped her down from the horse. Standing on shaky legs, she waited while he untied the rag and pulled it from her mouth. As soon as the stuffing was removed, all the anxiety, the terror, everything came spilling out. While Lewis slipped his coat around her shoulders, Charity gave her assailant an earful.

"Yes, that's right, you tell them why your employer wants me to return. Tell them the real reason you came after me," she yelled at the man, waiting for Lewis to untie her hands.

Once he did, anger raged through her and she strode over and kicked Mr. Devillin in the shin with all her strength. Before Lewis could stop her, she hit him with her fist. Pummeling him with her doubled up hands like a punching bag, the pain exploding in her numb hands.

"Get that bitch off me," he screamed.

Lewis grabbed her by the arms and she continued to yell at the man, fed up with being haunted by the wicked grotesque male, her Irish temper flaring, blazing hot like a forest fire. "I'm not going to be his whore. Never. It's not going to happen. And if I see your ugly face much more, you're going to find a bullet between your eyes. Don't you ever come near me again."

As she whirled around to face her husband, Lewis stared at her, a grin on his face. "Mrs. Huntington, remind me to never make you angry. You've got a mean temper."

Throwing her arms around her husband, she clung to Lewis and kissed him full on the mouth. Abruptly, they released, and she stared into his eyes, never wanting to let him go. "I've never been so afraid. He threatened to shoot you. You don't threaten my family. You're mine."

Lewis held her tightly in his arms and patted her on the back. "You're mine, as well. No one takes or harms what belongs to me."

LEWIS WAS BEGINNING to feel frightened. Last night when he learned Charity had been kidnaped, he'd never experienced such rage. The urge to beat the man who dared take his wife filled him with fury. Then when she told him she tried to protect him, his chest nearly burst with emotion. How did he handle his growing feelings for Charity?

Last night, he brought his wife home and showed her the only way he could with his actions, the words he couldn't say.

Now this morning, they worked side by side in the saloon and he didn't want to let her out of his sight. In fact, at first, he refused to let her come down.

Somehow she wrapped her arms around him, pressed her naked body against his and gave him a look with her emerald eyes that had him giving her anything she wanted.

And he hated feeling vulnerable. Charity, he feared, had the ability to shatter his heart. No woman before ever made him so defenseless. Like she stormed the walls of the castle and he yelled surrender. Now he worried that if she left him, he would be devastated. There were secrets between them that could send her running.

The sheriff strolled through the door. "Good morning, I need to talk with you two about Mr. Devillin's claims."

Quinn seemed like a decent honest man and Lewis liked

him. They even traded war stories, each man talking about what division they were in and their overall thoughts on the Great War. Yet, Lewis was leery of the sheriff. How would Quinn react when the truth about Lewis's identity was revealed?

"Good morning, Sheriff. Why didn't you bring Sarah," Charity asked as she walked into the room, her arms loaded with clean glasses. Setting the tray on the counter, she walked over to the man.

"This is official business and I need to ask you some questions," he said.

"Sure," she said. "Anything to keep that ingrate behind bars."

"Tell me your side of the story," Quinn said.

All three sat at the table together. What if there was something Charity kept from him about her reasons for coming to Angel Creek. With her auburn hair and sultry emerald eyes, he understood his wife was a spitfire. Why did the man come searching for her?

"Mr. Devillin said he came to collect from you because you owe Mr. Roberts money. Is this true?"

Chastity's brows rose and she stared at the sheriff. "This is the first I've heard that I owe him money. When I couldn't pay the taxes on my family home, he bought our estate from the county. Why would I be indebted to the man?"

"He said something about the inside of the house being vandalized. Do you know anything about the house being damaged?"

Sitting beside him, Lewis felt his wife tense. "The morning I left to catch the train to come here, along with the other brides, the house had a little damage. What house in the south, doesn't have damage from the war? Besides, what happened to it after I left is his problem. By that time, it was his property."

Why did Lewis think his wife was lying? Could her little destruction mean the inside was ragged? His wife had a temper. Lord help who she set her sights on, including him.

"Maybe he's talking about the fancy dress he sent over for me to wear the night he planned on auctioning me off to the men who visited his brothel. If tearing a dress to shreds is considered vandalism, yes, I'm guilty. Because I left that silk garment in tatters. My way of telling him I would never work for him. Ever."

The sheriff snickered and glanced at Lewis who shook his head. Oh yes, his wife probably ripped up everything in that house. What a mess the man must have walked in to find.

"You see, Mr. Roberts purchased that place with the purpose of turning my beloved home into a whore-house. Since he owns the place, he can do whatever he wants with it, but that purchase did not include me." She shivered. "Even if I continued living in my home, it would never be the same."

Why had she never told him about the brothel owner trying to recruit her? Was this the reason she left Charleston in a hurry?

"That's all you did? Sounds to me he was coercing a woman against her will into prostitution which is against the law."

Lewis watched his wife's expressive face, noticing the way she licked her lips and looked away. Oh yes, she did more than just rip the gown up. Knowing his rebel Irish spitfire, the inside of the house probably matched the silken garment.

"Well, I knocked a few holes in the bedroom plaster. The thought of what he intended to do in those rooms left me angry. My beautiful family home was being turned into a place of ill repute and it made me sick. He's lucky, I don't know witchcraft or I would have put a spell on the house."

If the situation hadn't been so serious, Lewis would have laughed. One thing was for certain, his life with Charity would never be boring.

The sheriff shook his head. "Do you want to press charges? We would have to go through the whole ordeal of a trial. Or I can escort him to the edge of town and tell him to never set foot in Angel Creek again."

The man looked toward Lewis for guidance, but he was smarter than to make his wife's decision.

"It's Charity's choice," Lewis said. "She decides the outcome for her kidnapper. But if she lets him go and he comes after her a second time, he's a dead man."

"I'm going to pretend you never said that, Lewis, but I understand your reaction."

They would need to be careful and make sure everything was secure so this character didn't find an easy opportunity to steal his wife again. Yesterday, the man received a taste of how his wife would never leave willingly.

Unless Mr. Devillin was prepared to deal with a hell cat for over a thousand miles, Lewis wasn't sure he would return. This morning, the man probably sported a well justified shiner.

Charity bit her lip. "Let him go, but tell Mr. Roberts I owe him nothing. After all, he took my home. He threatened my reputation. If he comes after me again, I'll write the newspaper and tell them how he tried to make me into one of his girls. How he's probably trying to do the same thing to other women."

Lewis smiled. His wife was not afraid of anything. Without a doubt, he knew the destruction had been more extensive than she let on. But the man deserved whatever retribution she gave him.

AFTER THE SHERIFF LEFT, Charity turned to see Lewis staring at her, a big grin on his face. "So, you left some holes in the walls of the bedrooms to show this Roberts fellow?"

A giggle erupted from her. The damage must have been extensive.

"Let's just say it was a very satisfying evening. Letting out all my frustrations about the war, my parents' deaths and the invitation to work in his brothel. All that anger I put into the swing of the hammer as I hit the walls. That plaster residue was everywhere. When I started, I never imagined I would make such a mess."

Lewis threw back his head and laughed. "Oh, Charity, remind me to never cross you."

"Why?" she asked innocently. Of course, she lost her temper, but never had she done anything so outrageous in all her life. Yet that night, she felt at peace, and filled with satisfaction the next morning as she closed the door on her family home for the last time.

New plaster would be required in certain rooms before they could conduct their naughty business. New furniture and even new paintings. The man said he wanted to redo the house and she gave his reconstruction a head start.

"Normally, I'm easy to get along with. If he just bought the house and not tried to buy me along with it, things would have been fine. To think I would entertain men for money brought out the Irish in me."

Her husband pulled her into his arms. "I'm grateful you answered the ad and came to me. Thank you for trying to protect me, but I can take care of myself."

And she knew he could as she reached out and stroked his handsome face. "No, we take care of each other. Until death do us part."

His lips covered hers and she melted into his embrace as his mouth promised her moments of pleasure in his arms later that night. At the sound of the back door closing, they broke apart.

When she glanced up, she saw Isaac standing in the back of the saloon. Stepping out of her husband's arms, she hated the separation, but she needed to talk to the boy.

"Isaac," she called.

"You're back. They found you."

She grinned at the young man. "Thanks to you. Thank you so much for helping me."

Last night, Lewis had told her the boy risked the wrath of Alice, trying to attract his attention. Because of Isaac, they found her much quicker than if he thought she went upstairs.

"He didn't hurt you?" Isaac asked, his eyes large in his skinny face. "Bad men killed my mom and pop."

Walking to him, she touched the young man on the arm. "Thanks to your quick thinking. Lewis was able to save me. Have you had lunch yet?"

"No," the boy said, his eyes widening.

Lewis stepped up to the young man. "You've asked to come work for me several times and I always said no. Not because I didn't think you weren't capable, but because I feared you would be too influenced by the alcohol. Some men make it appear like drinking is a great life and I want you to know it's not."

Her husband paused, and Charity held her breath hoping this meant what she hoped. "I'd like to offer you a job with the promise that you will attend school during the day and then in the afternoons and evenings you'll work here."

Charity's pulse leaped with excitement. Why did she feel so blessed to have chosen to leave Charleston and found Angel Creek? The boy needed a place indoors to sleep. "You can sleep in the work area in the closet. I'll find you a mattress. After we buy a house, you could move into the apartment over the saloon."

Nodding, Lewis smiled at Charity.

The boy stared at them, his mouth open in shock. "A place to bed down out of the cold and a job?"

"Yes," Charity said, "and you start tonight. There is a lot of trash out there to burn. Later there will be dirty dishes to clean."

Impulsively, he leaned over and hugged Charity. "That man

scared me. Mrs. Charity, I was so afraid for you. Now because I helped you, I've got a job and a place to sleep."

"Don't forget school," Lewis said. "We want you to go to school."

The young man nodded. "Yes, sir."

"Dinner is at four, before we get busy. We'll see you then."

"Yes, ma'am, and thank you. No one's done anything nice like this for me since my parents died. Thank you."

The boy ran out the door and Charity turned to her husband and slipped into his arms. "Thank you. He's a good kid whose life bestowed a difficult hand. You won't be sorry."

"If not for him, I wouldn't have known what happened to you. And the boy suffered because he came inside to tell me. Alice dealt that kid a blow. As of today, she no longer works for us. It seemed Alice aided Mr. Devillin by telling you that Isaac was waiting outdoors. That was the final straw."

A shiver trickled down Charity's spine. Between Alice and Mr. Devillin, she would have found herself back in Charleston, on her back in her own home. Thank goodness Isaac told Lewis.

"Always remember I will never leave without saying goodbye."

"Me too," Lewis said holding her in his arms.

CHAPTER 9

That night like every night for the past week, Lewis watched his wife handle the men in the saloon. By now she knew many of the regulars' names.

"Hi, George, how are the kids? Did little Billie get over his cold?" she asked the man and Lewis heard him tell her all about his son's symptoms and how he was getting over the sickness.

When Alice came into work earlier in the day, he'd given her the money he owed her and told her she was fired. The woman had been stunned, but when she tried to cozy up with him, he should have sent her packing right then.

After he confronted her about punching the boy, she told him she helped Mr. Devillin so Charity would no longer be here and they could be together. The rage he felt at that moment had him ordering her to leave and never come back.

At that moment, he realized she would never accept he didn't want her. Never had and never would. Not the kind of life he wanted.

Now his only waitress was his wife and that left him nervous. Not because she couldn't manage the clientele, but fearful of his reaction. Any man daring to look at her wrong, a fight would be on his hands and he would find himself in the street, in the dirt.

One of the men who searched for her came in the door.

"James," she called, "what would you like to drink?"

The man gazed at her in a way that reflected concern for her safety and health. "You good? That man didn't hurt you, did he? If he did, I'll help Lewis kill him."

"Oh, James," she said with a smile. "I don't know if I should thank you for offering to kill a man for me, but I'm fine. Don't worry about him. On his ride out of town, he's sporting a black eye. In fact, come to find out he was wanted."

Several hours ago, Quinn returned to tell them the choice was out of their hands. Wanted for murder, the man would be leaving in a prison wagon. The man would be incarcerated for a long time and Lewis couldn't be happier.

"Well, he should be hung. In our community, we don't want men who try to harm women. Tell Lewis I'm here if he needs my help."

Lewis listened to his wife talk to James and wasn't jealous. No flirtation went on between the two, just two friends making certain one had not been harmed.

Because of his wife's sweet, caring nature, sales continued to increase. Men in town liked him, but when someone showed interest in their family life or paid attention to why they sat there drinking, they adored her. Charity was the reason the business boomed.

Lonely men gravitated toward her smile and the way she genuinely cared about their lives and happiness. In the short time she'd been here, she turned patrons into friends.

"It was so nice of you to help Lewis find me. Especially since your wife was feeling poorly. Is she doing any better?"

How many times had Alice asked about a customer's family? How their wife was doing or even their own wellbeing? In the months she worked here, he never heard her inquire about anything personal. Just took the money.

James sighed. "No, I'm really worried about her. I've hired a woman to take care of her until she's better. **The** only reason I came in tonight is to check on you and to find out what happened. Now I need to get home to be with her."

His wife leaned forward and said softly, "I'll keep your wife in my prayers."

The man looked like he wanted to cry. "Thank you. That means a lot."

"How many years have you two been married," Charity asked stepping back.

"Soon be twenty-five. My life would be so empty without her. That's why I had to help you and Lewis. Though you haven't been together long, from watching the two of you, I can see how sweet you are on each other."

Lewis had been eavesdropping to hear what Charity and the man were talking about, and he froze on the inside. Was it that obvious the two of them were starting to fall for one another? He glanced up and stared into Charity's emerald eyes and felt a zing of awareness seize his stomach and chest.

Charity smiled at him, her full lips so welcoming and inviting, he longed to kiss her. All he could do was dream about them, and know just as soon as they closed, he would have her in his arms again. Glancing over, he noticed her tip jar and already it was halfway full.

"Thanks, James. And thank you for coming to my rescue last night. Lewis and I hope we can be as happy and be married as long as you and your wife."

Is that what Lewis wanted? Originally he only planned on being married for the thirty days, but now he didn't want the marriage to end. But would his wife love him when she found out about his birth? What about his secret? Would she love him when she learned the truth?

~

SINCE THE KIDNAPPING, Charity had never been happier. Every day she fell more and more in love with her husband and the nights she spent in his arms. Working in the saloon became more of a joy than a nuisance and the two of them were building their life together.

She hadn't told Lewis, but she was saving her tip money for them to buy a little house in town. Every day she took her coins to the bank and exchanged them for dollar bills that she hid throughout the books pages.

Their new home didn't need to be large, just a little two-bedroom cottage where they could begin their family.

Today, she and Isaac were going to surprise Lewis, who left to run errands. While he was gone, Isaac brought in the little pine tree he'd cut and they put it in a corner. Some men who came to the Angel Creek Palace had no one to spend the holidays with.

This was her small way of making certain they experienced a little of the Christmas spirit.

"Hang that tinsel over the bar," she told Isaac who was standing on a ladder in front of the mirror hanging on the back wall.

"Mrs. Charity, there's not going to be enough."

"Oh, yes, there will be. Now dip the tinsel and bring it back up," she coached the boy.

Christmas was only a week away and she couldn't believe they had already been married almost thirty days. A month had passed and she had yet to start her monthly flow. They had only been having marital relations for two weeks, but she was past due already.

Could be the stress of moving from her homeland, cross-country travel, and starting a new life, but she was late.

Time would tell if she was expecting and the thought filled

her with so much excitement. Having a baby with Lewis would be so wonderful. She was afraid of being disappointed, so she tried not to concentrate on the possibility. Right now, she needed to focus on decorating the saloon for Christmas before he returned.

"That's perfect," she said, beaming at the young man. "Now help me put mistletoe over the doorway and I think we're all done."

Isaac carried the ladder over to the entrance where he hung a piece of the plant over the swinging doors. Because of the cold weather, years ago, a small entryway had been built, so that two doors led into the saloon. One from the outside that kept the cold from spilling into the bar.

"What are you going to do for Christmas?" she asked the boy.

He shrugged and looked away. "Nothing."

"Aren't you going to the town gathering at the church on Christmas Eve? Go with us."

The boy glanced away. "As the town beggar, you're not really invited to parties or gatherings."

But by the grace of God, that could have been her. Her own life almost became like Isaac's. "Well, I would love if you would attend the party with Mr. Lewis and myself. You are welcome to join us for Christmas dinner. Who knows, Santa might bring a present for you."

The kid looked back at her, his face was a mixture of emotions, his eyes flashing. "Why are you so nice to me? Do you feel sorry for me? Is it pity?"

Shaking her head, she placed an ornament on the Christmas tree. Simple decorations she made from paper and glue, but they festooned the tree. "Of course not. Did you know that both of my parents and my only brother died during the war? My home was auctioned off because of delinquent taxes? A man tried to coerce me into working at a brothel?"

This holiday was the first she'd felt hopeful in a long

time. Turning, she faced him, wanting him to experience some hope for the future. "When I look at you, I see a kid who is going to be a strong man someday.

"Right now, he needs a little help. Everyone could use a little assistance occasionally. My friends are the ones who gave me the courage to leave Charleston. If not for them, I probably would have stayed and been forced out on the street, like you."

Sometimes when she closed her eyes to go to sleep, she marveled at how she almost didn't come to Angel Creek. How torn she felt leaving her home behind. How disgusted she would have been to watch the place she loved turned into a whorehouse.

Sure there would be tough times, but here she had Lewis and friends and Isaac.

"We have a lot in common."

"Yes, we do, Isaac. And no, I don't pity you. Though I never actually lived on the street, I came close. So I understand a little bit about what you went through. More importantly, I want to help you the way my friends helped me. Someday when you get the opportunity, you should lift someone in need. Do you understand?"

Even if it wasn't the holidays, she would still help people when she could. For every blessing she gave, she received it back tenfold.

The kid smiled at her. "Yes, ma'am, I do. I'll think about the town celebration and let you know. But I will come to Christmas lunch."

"Good, we'd love to have you."

This year would be different. Their first Christmas as a married couple.

As they finished, she stood back and stared at the decorations. "What do you think?"

"I ain't never seen a prettier tree," he said, gazing at it in wonder. "The last tree I had was the year my parents were killed."

"Memories of past Christmas times are always with us. It's time we made some new memories, Isaac. Both of us need new happy times, not to forget, but rather to fill us with happiness."

The boy reached out and touched her on the arm. "Thank you, Mrs. Charity, for all you've done."

Tears welled up in her eyes. The kid just needed some help like she did in getting out of Charleston.

"You're welcome, Isaac. Now before you make me start bawling, I've got to run an errand. Mr. Frank's sister is feeling poorly, and I want to take her a dish I made for them to eat. Tell Lewis I'll be back soon. Make sure your homework is done."

"Yes, ma'am."

IN THE MERCANTILE, the woman handed him the latest letter.

"Pretty fancy, Lewis. Your father rich?"

Lewis stared at the envelope, his stomach tightening into a nauseous ball of nerves. "You might say that."

He walked away from the woman and her prying eyes, fearing what was contained in this missive.

A second letter from Jakob's father. What should he do?

Ripping open the seal, he pulled out the parchment paper. Slowly, he read the words, his heart pounding in his chest, his blood rushing through him as he stared at the ink.

Dear son,

I know that we parted on less than happy terms, but I thought after I sent you the mail-order bride, I would hear from you. My solicitor informed me business in the bar has never been better and I'm so pleased with how you took my advice.

Christmas will be here soon and I would hope that somehow we could mend our relationship. Maybe even spend the holidays togeth-

er. I'm anxiously awaiting hearing from you. Please respond as soon as
possible. Let's put the past in the past and concentrate on the future.

Your mother would have wanted us to be close.

Your Loving Father,

Thomas Huntington

What did Lewis do? Did he reply or did he come clean and
tell him the truth? So many decisions and now he had to not
only think of himself, but also, Charity. What affected him also
affected her.

Who was the solicitor in town telling Mr. Huntington how
well the saloon had been doing? Surely, there was some way to
learn who the rat was and tell him to stop.

If the man showed up, he could lose everything. Yet if he
responded to the correspondence, he would come running. The
man was no fool and would recognize the handwriting was not
Jakob's. Only a couple hundred dollars more and he would offer
to purchase the business. Soon.

Stepping out into the sunshine, he walked over to a trash
barrel, pulled out some matches from his pocket and struck one
against a rock. In a matter of seconds, the paper caught fire and
burned until the wind blew wisps of the ashes away.

As he stared down the street at the saloon, he couldn't help
but think about his wife. An innocent who didn't deserve to be
entangled in his deception. Lewis ran his hands through his
hair, torn about what to do. Life had given him a second
chance. An opportunity and he'd taken advantage of it.

He walked across the street heading home to the woman
who if he hadn't become Jakob Lewis Huntington, he never
would have met. Now he couldn't imagine being without her
and the business he loved. At least until it all blew up.

CHAPTER 10

*S*omething bothered Lewis, and Charity had no clue what could be wrong. After he came back from his errands this afternoon, he'd barely acknowledged the Christmas decorations. Even when she told him that Isaac helped her, he didn't say much.

As the evening crowds began to come in, Lewis received a lot of ribbing from the regulars. "Lewis, your wife is making you sentimental. Next thing, you'll be decorating for Valentine's Day."

These men needed to understand celebrations of any kind brought them closer together. Now she might decorate for Valentine's Day. Why not?

"Shut up, Joe, that might happen. When was the last time you bought your wife a Christmas present?" Charity asked.

"Uh, the first year we married," he said sheepishly.

What else had the man not celebrated? Their anniversary?

"Stop complaining your wife is not romantic. The problem might not all be her. Have you tried being a little more caring?" Charity asked. "Like going home early and helping her with the kids for starters."

"You kicking me out of here?" he asked.

"Not unless you get drunk and then you will find yourself in the street."

Since Charity became the full-time barmaid, Lewis didn't allow drunks to remain. If they became inebriated, Lewis escorted them to the door and sent the men on their way.

From behind the bar, Lewis spoke up. "Be careful, Joe. 'Tis the season to be merry, just not drunk."

Charity moved down the counter handing out drinks and saying hello to their clients. So many lonely men and while she felt for them, she knew her boundaries. Lewis made her happy. Now she needed to figure out what troubled him.

"Are you Charity?"

At the sound of the man's voice, she turned to face a new client. "Yes, I am. What can I do for you?"

"I wanted to tell you thank you. This afternoon you delivered dinner to my sister's family and we appreciate it so much."

The fact the man came into the saloon to thank her warmed her heart. "Your sister is in my prayers. Truly, I hope she gets better. It was an honor to be able to help."

The man smiled. A handsome young man, it saddened her, he was dealing with such a terrible situation. To watch a family member suffer for months and slowly waste away was a horrible time for any family.

"Anyway, I wanted to come in and say thank you."

"Merry Christmas," she said to him. "Let me know if I can do anything else."

The man turned and walked out the door.

Suddenly Lewis appeared at her side. "Do you know who that is?"

"No, I took his sister's family food for tonight. We had plenty and she was ill, so I wanted to help."

Years ago, her mother had always taken food to a family who either suffered a death or an illness and Charity went with her. Once when they returned home, she asked her mother why she did this. And her mother responded, to help families while their loved ones were ill was her mission.

Her way of serving people who were suffering. From the time she had been a little girl that stayed with Charity and when she moved here, she decided to carry on her mother's tradition.

Lewis whispered in her ear. "That man is the governor's son. He must be visiting in town for the holidays."

"Well, good, I wanted to help that poor family out. The sister doesn't look well."

Joe leaned toward both of them. "The governor has nothing to do with his daughter. Said she married beneath her and deserves whatever she receives."

Charity realized her father would probably think she'd married beneath her, but he wasn't here, and neither was her mother. After the war, that nonsense no longer mattered. And Lewis, her kind man was winning her heart. Social status didn't matter when it came to finding the right man and she believed she found the perfect man for herself.

"If she loved the man she married, then she won't care what others think. What they have together is all that's impor-tant." Locating her husband across the room, she smiled at him. "Like my man."

Someday soon she would tell him she had fallen in love with him, but not in public. That would be a private moment between the two of them. The moment she would cherish and cling to until the day she died.

"Wish my wife would say things like that to me."

"Maybe she would if you remained at home."

Joe grinned. "Hell fire, woman, I'm taking the hint. I'm going home to spend time with my wife."

The man was nice, just not very intelligent when it came to women. Hopefully she aided him in seeing why his wife was so upset when he came home late after leaving her with the children.

"Smart man. Buy her a Christmas gift. See you the next time you come in, Joe," she said, watching the man leave.

No sooner had he walked out the door than Charity noticed Lewis watching her closely. She winked at him, flirting outrageously, wishing it was closing time and they were alone. Yes, she was in love with her husband.

CHARITY SAT around the quilting frame Sarah had found hidden in a closet. Once again, the women tried to meet on a regular basis when they had time and the weather cooperated.

Today, Ruby and Julia were missing. Ruby because she was out of town, and Julia because of the snow. Staring at her friends, she felt like her life had come full circle, only now instead of being discouraged, Charity was happy.

"Look, we're quilting again," Charity said, smiling and laughing.

"Yes, we're back together, except for the two others. Ruby is still off with her husband, fighting that disease. Does anyone know when they'll be back?" Anna asked.

"No," Sarah said, pulling a needle through the material of the quilt.

While she missed seeing her friends, she understood the important work they were doing. Still, since the move, they weren't as close, but were blessed to all be together.

"Though I was the one who purchased the Groom's Gazette, I never would have had the courage to leave without each of you by my side," Charity said, gazing at Anna and Sarah. "I'm so glad we did this together. What about you? Are you happy we left Charleston?"

Sarah smiled. "Yes, this was my only hope of keeping my daughter at my side."

Since the death of her first husband in the Great War, Sarah and Becca had been through so much. At least here, Sarah didn't need to worry about the in-laws any longer.

"I can't believe you ladies talked me into going on this adventure with you. Here it is almost Christmas, and it's so much better than being where we lost everything," Anna said with a smile. "There's hope we're all going to find love."

For Charity, she knew she loved Lewis and was waiting for the right moment to tell her husband. Plus, every day she grew more confident she was expecting.

"So what are you each getting your husbands for Christmas?" Sarah asked.

The women glanced at her.

"Christmas is next week. You're running out of time to either make or purchase something for your new husband," Charity said wondering what her friends were thinking.

Sometime in the next few days, she had to sneak out and go shopping for her husband and Isaac. The boy was becoming a part of their family, often having dinner with them. The kid needed someone to care about him and Lewis and she were growing attached to him.

In the afternoons, Lewis had been helping him with his schoolwork, trying to bring the boy up to the right grade level for his age.

"Something for his favorite horse, Jack. That man loves that animal," Sarah said with a sigh. "He's my biggest competition."

The women giggled.

"Do you have any suggestions? I don't have a clue. What about you," Anna said. "What are you going to buy Lewis?"

"A wedding ring. If I can find one I can afford. New clothes for Isaac, so he doesn't look like a beggar. The boy hasn't had anything but hand-me-downs for so long."

The boy was not big enough for Lewis's clothes and too big for his own now that he was filling out from eating properly, seemed tighter and shorter. He would soon outgrow all of what he wore.

"You've really have taken that child under your wing," Sarah replied, not looking up but putting in her tiny stitches.

And Charity had. Everything in her screamed that could have been her so easily, living on the streets, begging for food.

"If we hadn't come to Angel Creek, we might all be homeless."

The women sighed.

"Yes, I needed this chance at happiness," Sarah said. "Life is not perfect here, but if we stayed in Charleston, life would be much worse."

Charity smiled at the women she grew up with, gone through a war with, and now found husbands through a newspaper. What a story they would tell their children someday.

"I'm late," she said, glancing at her friends. "Don't know if it means anything, but I'm about two weeks late."

"Our thirty days are not up," Anna said. "Have you?"

"Yes," Charity said with a giggle. "We didn't wait."

"But, Charity, you can't back out now. You're committed to being married to Lewis for the rest of your life. Is that what you want?" Anna asked.

For a moment, she sat and thought about their life together. A kind-hearted man with a caring soul who would protect her and their children; their future together seemed perfect.

Yes, she wanted to remain married to him for the rest of her life. Bear his children, create a home, and love him until she took her last breath. "Most definitely, I'm in love with my man. Lewis is honest and good and everything I could want in a husband."

"Even though he owns a saloon?" Anna asked shocked.

"Funny thing, I love working beside him in the bar. So many

lonesome men who just come in to drink and be around people. What this town needs is a matchmaker. Someone to find ladies for these lonely hearts."

Sarah tilted her head and smiled at her. "That would be appropriate for you. Maybe if the saloon doesn't work out, you should think about setting up a shop and finding women for the men in town."

Making her stitches smooth, she pondered the idea of matchmaking some of the men she met. Oh yes, she could do this. Working at the saloon, she heard a lot about their lives. All the disappointments, their frustrations, and even their confessions about women they loved and lost.

When the time came, this might be something for her to consider.

"Lewis runs a clean establishment and working beside him, I've learned so much about life and men and how they think. Most of them are just big ole teddy bears."

A laugh bubbled up from her chest. "There are some that are stubborn and bull-headed who had to experience being tossed out in the street. My husband makes it clear, I belong to him and no one touches or treats his wife badly without suffering the consequences."

The day she decorated the saloon for the holidays, she noticed something bothered him. Something he refused to talk about. Sooner or later, she would learn his secret and when she did they would solve it together.

"I love my husband very much, but I'm waiting to tell him. By Christmas I may know if I'm expecting. This year is going to be the best holiday ever."

"Charity, I'm thrilled for you," Sarah said.

"The first one of us to expect a baby. After Charleston, I'm so happy for you," Anna said. "In fact, I wish it were me."

Thomas Huntington waited months to hear from his son Jakob. His son beyond spoiled, he'd done his best to try to make him into a man. Purchasing him a saloon and sending him a mail-order bride. This time, he had high hopes his son would take the steps to finally settle down.

After months of no correspondence, he made the decision to travel from California to find out for himself how Jakob faired. Even battling a snowstorm between Idaho and Montana. Hours and hours on horseback and a guide who charged him extra for coming in winter. The trek across miles of mountains was not for the faint of heart.

Never again would he make this journey in summer, let alone while it was cold.

Four days before Christmas, he sat in the saloon glancing around at the establishment he owned. For a Thursday evening, the place was packed with men drinking, Christmas decorations hanging on the walls to remind them of the season. Why did he feel like Ebenezer Scrooge coming to disrupt the party?

"What can I get for you, sir? This must be your first time as I don't remember seeing you before," the pretty waitress asked him.

The look he gave her should have scared her away, but she smiled and stood patiently. "Whiskey."

At least his son had great taste in the barmaids he hired. If they could convince her to dance on a stage, they'd be packing the house every night.

"Coming right up."

She turned to walk away and he grabbed her arm and whirled her around.

Facing him, she gave him a stern glance. "Sir, do not touch me unless you want my husband to throw you out into the street."

That stunned him as he glanced around. The woman was a barmaid. A whore who should be accustomed to being touched by the men ordering drinks. Hell, she should be dancing, drawing an even bigger crowd.

"Sorry, I wanted to ask you a question. When will Jakob Huntington be in?"

Thomas watched her as his eyes narrowed, her brows drew together. "Jakob, or Lewis, as we call him, is behind the counter."

"Lewis?" he said bewildered. "I don't see him."

Why would they call Jakob, Lewis? That wasn't his name. Only one man stood behind the bar and he wasn't Jakob.

"Yes, Jakob Lewis Huntington is the handsome man standing behind the bar, giving you the evil eye. My husband doesn't approve of any man touching me."

Her husband? What the hell was going on here? Could this woman be the bride he ordered for his son?

"Excuse me, I'll bring you your drink," she said, walking away, leaving a very dumbfounded Thomas staring at the man, wondering what he had done with Jakob.

Something was afoot just like he suspected. For that man certainly was not his son, Jakob Huntington.

As he started to rise and walk over to the counter, something held him back. Time to do a little more investigating before he let the man know the ruse was up. But where was Jakob.

What had the man done with his boy? Or did he go traipsing off to the gold fields like he wanted. Yet the man used his son's name. What happened to his boy?

CHAPTER 11

*T*he next morning, Thomas went to the bank. He owned the saloon and the accounts created belonged to him. Therefore, all the money the business earned, should be his, not this imposter's. Walking into the establishment, he faced the teller.

"My name is Thomas Huntington, owner of the Angel Palace Saloon. I'm here to close the account."

The man's mouth fell open. "Lewis owns the saloon."

"Check the details. My solicitor, Wilson Randolph, set the account up under my name. He keeps me informed as to what is happening at the saloon, where my son is the manager."

One way to bring Jakob out of hiding or make this character portraying him realize he knew the truth would be to squeeze the purse strings. When he pulled the money out, there would be no cash to run the business. No cash would bring Jakob running to him.

The man checked the file and then came back to the window. "Mr. Huntington, I'll take care of that for you."

"How much did my son make?" he asked.

The clerk glanced at him, his mouth thinning into a straight line. "Almost ten thousand dollars."

"My son has done very well."

But it wasn't his son. No, it was some man named Lewis that he had no clue about. The man was obviously business savvy as he'd turned his investment into a nice profit.

If Jakob didn't come see him in the next day, he would contact the sheriff and close the saloon. Whether he continued to let this con artist run the business depended on what he learned about his son. Right now, he was leaning toward closing it forever.

The banker counted out his money.

Once he was done, he slid the bills toward him. "This closes this account."

Thomas picked up the bundles and stuffed them into his pockets and walked out of the bank, his business completed. The imposter would have quite a surprise waiting for him.

CHARITY WOKE EARLY the next morning curled around her husband. He snuggled deeper into her embrace. "Good morning."

"Good morning, sunshine," he said, kissing the tip of her nose.

The mornings in bed with her husband were the best, lazily spent beside one another. They slept later than most couples because by the time they closed the saloon, it was late.

"Christmas is only a few days away," she said, gazing into his indigo eyes.

"And what do you want for Christmas," he asked her.

There were really only two things she wanted as she gazed at him. "A wedding ring and a house."

"What bank do you want me to rob to fulfill your wishes?"

Since she had only lived in one house, she had no idea the cost of a home, but surely eventually they could afford a small place to call their own.

A giggle erupted from her and she relished the security she always felt in his arms. "No bank robbery. Maybe a ring. Someday, I would love for us to buy a house. Someplace where our children can grow up."

There was no way she wanted their children to live over a saloon. In the weeks since she started working there, she knew it was not a bad place, but kids needed a safe environment where they could go outside. A place where they could walk to school.

"I agree. Right now, I don't think that's going to be possible," he said.

Once again, she was getting a feeling something wasn't right. "Is everything fine? You've acted worried lately and I hope I'm not the reason you're worrying."

Lewis rolled her beneath him and stared down at her, his body pressing into hers. "You are the bright spot in my life. Though I have to admit sometimes chasing after you and keeping you out of trouble is quite a handful."

Staring into his large sapphire eyes, she thought about saying she loved him, but decided to wait. What better time to tell him than Christmas morning when she gave him his ring.

"Me, a handful? How can that be?" she said, teasing him. "I'm an innocent."

"Until you get angry, and then, look out. Thank goodness, you haven't been mad at me yet. One day, I'm sure I'll experience your wrath."

What her husband didn't realize was that when she was hurt, she became distant and withdrawn. It was only when someone angered her, she reacted so strongly. Often times without even thinking, just reacting.

Grinning, she slipped her arms around his neck and smiled. "But right now, Irish eyes are smiling on you."

A groaned escaped from his throat as his lips covered her mouth as he kissed her thoroughly. With a sigh, she melted into his body. When their lips came apart, he looked down at her.

"Sometimes a man doesn't know how lonely he is until a woman comes along and shows him what he's missing. Don't ever think I'm not glad you came into my world. After the holidays, we're going to make plans for the future. At that time, we'll discuss buying a house."

Did he know how much he made her happy? Just considering the purchase let her know they planned on being together.

"Thank you, Lewis. A home filled with love and children and you are all I want," she said, knowing what a blessing coming to Angel Creek was.

"Me too," he said layering his mouth over her lips, once again.

An hour later, her husband left their small apartment to run some errands. While he was gone, she tidied up their living quarters and then went to her hidden stash of cash. Counting the money, she pulled out enough to do her shopping and headed out the door.

She couldn't wait for Christmas to arrive. At that time, she would tell her husband she loved him and she was almost certain they were expecting. Their first holiday together would be special, and she could hardly wait.

LEWIS SAT across from Isaac and listened to the boy read to him.

"The brown cat chased the mouse across the floor until it ran into a crack in the wall. Once again the mouse out..."

"Sound the word out," Lewis told the boy.

The kid looked up at him, frustration in his eyes. "Why are we doing this? I don't need to learn how to read."

"Keep working," Lewis said, patiently waiting for the kid to see he wasn't going anywhere until he figured out the word.

With a sigh, Isaac looked back at the text. "Sm-art-ed. Outsmarted the silly cat."

Not long after Isaac returned home from school one day, frustrated that the kids were making fun of his reading, Lewis started listening to him read. Since then, in the afternoons, he practiced with Lewis. Charity was right. Isaac needed their help.

"That's much better," Lewis said. "Reading will become easy once you practice it enough, the words flow automatically through your brain. In fact, my favorite book is upstairs. Once you learn to read, you can go to magical places. Remind me later and I'll bring it down for you."

Somehow he needed to interest the kid in learning how to read. Yes, life dealt him a blow he would never recover from, but even Lewis's father made certain he received an education. He wanted to do the same for Isaac. It was the way out of poverty.

"Maybe I don't want to read."

"So you care nothing about reading stories of pirates and soldiers and distant lands and kings."

The boy frowned. "Make believe isn't real."

"No, it's not. Sometimes it's fun to see how other people struggle and overcome problems. Things like death and war and being poor."

The boy's brows drew together. "Are there stories about orphans finding a family?"

Lewis's chest tightened, and he understood his anger. While growing up, he often felt lonely, even though his father and his legitimate children resided on the other side of town. Being the unwanted child, he could never mingle with his brothers and sisters. They probably didn't know he existed.

Books had taken him out of his world and put him in a place where he belonged.

"Yes, Isaac, there are orphan stories about getting new families and being accepted and loved."

The boy stared at him. "You're lucky to have your family."

If the kid knew his background, he would realize that Lewis had nothing. Only an overbearing father who wanted to sacrifice his sons to the United States military, especially the accidental son.

A laugh escaped from Lewis as he gazed at the boy. "To you it probably seems like I do, but my world is not perfect by any means. I was born the ill..."

How could he tell this boy he was no different from him? Because he was impersonating a man who came from a large wealthy family. Nothing like Lewis's reality.

"Always remember things may not be as they appear," he told the kid. "But don't ever give up on trying new things and finding out what makes you happy. Remember your past and try to help people when you can."

The boy's eyes darkened and he growled. "Why should I help people when they wouldn't help me?"

How long had the boy lived in the cold, hungry, wet, with no one that cared about him? The boy's pride kept him from accepting handouts, but it was understandable why he didn't want to help others.

"The very reason why you must become a better man than they are. There will come a time in life when you have the opportunity to help someone and then you remember the help you were given."

The boy was filled with hate at what life bequeathed him and Lewis felt his pain. The memory of how his father didn't want to accept him, but his conscious compelled him to at least send him to a military academy. The boy's parents were killed in some kind of robbery and he was forced to roam the streets.

In many ways, their lives were similar.

Until Lewis and Charity had taken him in and given him a place to sleep and a job.

"You keep reading so you can grow into an honorable, educated man. Make something of yourself and show the people who never helped you they missed their chance."

That seemed to perk the boy up.

"I'll get that book for you."

When he came back down, he handed the book to Isaac. "This book is my favorite, so I want it back. Now I've got to get to the mercantile before they close. Christmas Eve is the day after tomorrow and I want to buy Charity's gift."

Hurrying out o tthe store, he thought about his wife. He'd almost told her he loved her this morning as they lay in bed like two kids laughing and giggling. She was the best thing that ever happened to him, but she deserved to know the truth.

After Christmas, he planned on telling Charity everything. Who he really was, how she changed him and made him into a man who wanted a family. And his biggest secret, he would tell her about his parentage and pray she would accept him.

CHAPTER 12

*T*he night before Christmas Eve, the saloon was having a party and then would close for two days, not reopening until the day after the holiday. Charity looked forward to having some time off to spend with Lewis and Isaac.

Almost running, she hurried, checking the decorations one last time. This afternoon she made a special punch, had cookies delivered from the bakery in town, and even made homemade eggnog.

Under the tree were presents to give away. Across the room, she setup a box for charitable giving. The sign said for the McGregor family.

Florence McGregor needed to see a doctor in San Francisco and she wanted to help the family by paying for the journey. Maybe not all of it, but at least a portion.

Watching Lewis preparing the bar for tonight, her heart filled with joy. In the last month, his revenues had increased and she liked to think she played a part in the rise in sales.

"Have you seen Isaac?"

"No," he said.

"Usually I see him before now," she said. "You don't think he's in any kind of trouble do you?"

"He's a big boy who can take care of himself," he told her.

Wanting to be the first to put a donation in the box, Charity went up the stairs to their small living area. At the shelf, she reached for the book she hid her money in. The book was gone. Over a hundred dollars was stuffed inside that book and now it was missing.

It was all her cash. Everything. Panic gripped her as she ran back downstairs looking for Lewis.

"Lewis," she cried running into the saloon. "The book is gone."

"Yeah, I gave it to Isaac to read," he said calmly.

Tears welled up in her eyes as she threw her hands over her face, nausea gripping her stomach. "Did you look inside before you gave it to him? That's where I tucked away my tips. All the money I earned was in that book. There's over a hundred inside the pages."

The door opened and the first patrons entered the building.

Charity's chest tightened, her stomach growing queasy. Penniless once again. After leaving Charleston, she swore this would never happen a second time. She promised herself she would never go without money.

"It's all right," Lewis said obviously trying to calm her. "We'll find Isaac and ask for the money back. The boy may not know the cash is in the book."

"Then why is Isaac and my money gone," she said dejectedly. "Once again, I'm broke."

"Honey, I'll give you some money. Once we locate Isaac, I'll find out what happened to your money."

Why did it feel like she'd lost once again? Why did it seem like no matter what she did, she couldn't get ahead? Yes, her husband would make sure she had money, but it felt good to have her own. That cash gave her confidence instead of being dependent on her man.

More men poured in the door and she knew the time had come to get busy. Yes, she would earn more tips, but she would have to start over, saving. That money she hoped to use to help buy them a house.

A place where if she were pregnant, they could raise this baby. And she was pretty certain they were expecting. All the symptoms existed and yet she refused to be too giddy about the baby until she told Lewis.

Two hours later, the Angel Creek Palace was crowded with men celebrating the holidays. The eggnog was history, the spiced punch almost gone, and the cookies had been consumed by grown men who seemed so happy to taste Christmas sweets once again.

Charity flitted about the room, serving drinks, knowing this was the only Christmas some men would participate in.

The evening waned, and it was time to hold the drawing.

"Gentlemen," Charity called. "There are three packages under the tree. When you walked in the door, you should have received a slip of paper with a number on it. I'm going to have a volunteer pull a number out of this bowl and if your number is called, choose your package."

The men all scrambled to find their number.

Funny how adults became like children when presents were being given away. Most of these men were loners without anyone.

"Are you ready?" She waited a moment. "Joe, please draw the numbers."

The man reached into the bowl. "Number fifteen."

A yell came from the back of the room and a lanky cowboy walked over to where they had a tree with trimmings set up. Grabbing the present, he nodded his thanks and walked to the side.

The entire saloon anxiously watched as he ripped open the gift to find a pair of work gloves.

"Number five," Joe called.

A quiet little man who barely spoke to anyone ran to the tree and snatched up his wrapped package.

"And last, number twenty-two," Joe said amid a loud chorus of groans as an older man whooped and hollered rushing over to grab the last present.

"Merry Christmas, everyone," Charity said and went back to serving whiskey, celebrating that the first annual Christmas event had been a roaring success.

While they probably spent a little money on the desserts and punch and the gifts, the men more than repaid them by purchasing alcohol. So far, no one was stumbling around drunk.

Suddenly the door slammed open and the sheriff walked in with a portly austere looking man. The man she served the night before.

"The saloon is closed," Quinn announced.

Stunned, Charity stood staring at the lawman, wondering what had they done?

Lewis jumped the counter and started walking toward Quinn, Charity making her way over to the men.

"What's going on, Quinn?" he asked, stepping up next to the man. The crowd around them squeezed in tight to hear his reasons for their closing.

"This man says he owns the Angel Creek Palace and he wants to shut it down," he said.

Who was this guy and how could he even consider he owned their business?

"Who are you?" Lewis asked.

"Thomas Huntington and you are not my son Jakob."

A gasp escaped from Charity. The man had to be crazy? Maybe another Huntington?

124

"Let's talk in the office," Lewis replied, his face grim.

"Close down the saloon and then we'll talk," the man demanded and the urge to kick him on the shin almost overwhelmed her.

One look at Lewis confirmed her worst fears. Frightened for her husband, she glanced at him and he nodded, signaling for her to close the doors.

As she opened the doors wide and the clientele filed out, she wished them each a Merry Christmas, though inside her heart was breaking. What was going on? If Lewis wasn't Jakob Huntington, who was he?

This couldn't be true. There had to be some kind of mistake as Lewis would never lie to her.

Joe stopped at the door, took her hand and held it tightly. "Hang in there. Right now, I don't understand what's going on. But Lewis is a good man and he loves you very much. Don't give up on him."

Tears sprang to her eyes as her heart raced with a pain unlike anything she ever experienced. Impulsively she wrapped her arms around Joe and gave him a hug. "I just hope he's not in trouble."

What if her husband went to jail? What would she do?

LEWIS NOW UNDERSTOOD how a man facing a firing squad must've felt as he walked into the office and shut the door behind him. On the outside, he heard Charity hurrying out the last of their customers, possibly forever.

Quinn sat and leaned back.

"Did you take on Jakob Huntington's identity?" he asked.

Licking his lips nervously, Lewis looked at Mr. Huntington. "Your son was shot in a shootout in Leadville, Colorado, over a mining claim."

The man cursed. From watching the older man, Lewis knew so many things Jakob said about his father were true.

"At the gunfight, Jakob was seriously injured, but he managed to escape out of town to a little cabin I was staying in where he collapsed. For the next week, I tried to heal his wounds. Even fetched the doctor from town, but no matter what either one of us did, Jakob became worse. Eventually he passed away."

His dark eyes flashed with anger as he shook his head. "You can verify all this can't you?"

"Yes, the doctor and the sheriff of Leadville were aware of the gunfight in town."

"So how did you wind up with the saloon?" Quinn asked.

"While he was ill, Jakob told me about the Angel Creek Palace. Told me his father purchased it for him and if I wanted to, I could have the bar, but I would need to pretend I was him. At first, I refused. After he died, I decided why not."

It was only after he learned his father was sending a patrol after him, he assumed Jakob's name, but that was information they didn't need. Taking a deep breath to calm his nerves, he said, "So I came to Angel Creek and became Jakob Lewis Huntington."

Mr. Huntington scowled at him like he wanted to kill him.

Why had he finally found something he enjoyed doing, a great wife, and everything he wanted only to have it yanked out from under him again?

"Once I earned enough money, I planned on purchasing the business from you and letting you know about Jakob's death. The money in the bank should be enough to buy the business."

The man tensed but didn't say a word as his dark beady eyes seem to bore into Lewis's soul.

In some ways, he couldn't blame the man for hating him. After all, he impersonated his dead son, the very man who gave the business to him. Yet, Lewis had done everything he could to help Jakob live.

"Sheriff, tomorrow, I'd like a telegram sent to the Leadville sheriff and one to the doctor. I need verification this man didn't murder my boy just to get his hands on this saloon."

Lewis felt his insides twist into a knot. This was how it would always appear to a man like Mr. Huntington. Men like Lewis were just trash to his kind of people and always would be. Why did he expect anything different?

"Don't worry," Quinn said, reassuring the man. "There will be an investigation. I've got an army buddy who lives in the area."

Everything would now be lost, but he wanted to clear his name. "The doctor will confirm my story and I can tell you where I buried him, if you'd like to know."

The man's fist clenched. "I'm his father. Of course, I want to know." The old man sighed. "That boy would not grow up. He would not listen to me."

"Jakob was a greenhorn in a town of hotheads and scalawags all trying to earn a quick buck off gold."

Quinn glanced at Lewis. "Do you have any documentation stating he agreed to do this?"

After Jakob died, he'd realized he should have had him sign something saying he gave the business to Lewis, but he kept hoping the man would recover.

"No, he died before I took him up on the offer. After his death, I decided to come to Angel Creek and assume his name until I could purchase the saloon."

All for a new start, under a new name, in a new town. All to hide from his father instead of confronting him. Maybe the time had come to tell his father he was done. If he wasn't arrested.

The old man snorted. "You could be making up all of this. There is no way to learn for certain my son consented to give you this bar. And besides, I own the business, not

Jakob. This was his last chance to straighten up and he dies in a mining town shoot out. Or at least that's your story."

Lewis tried his best to understand the man's anger not only at his son, but also at him for lying. The man refused to acknowledge Lewis also tried to help his son heal.

"The doctor and I did everything to save Jakob. Enough men were killed in the war, I didn't want to watch another man slip away. After I made the decision to take his place, I had every intention of trying to purchase the saloon from you after Christmas. Working the business, I've earned enough money to buy it from you."

The old man grinned and a trickle of alarm grabbed Lewis by the throat. "The money the bar *I own* made?"

Without a doubt, Lewis perceived the truth. Somehow he needed to get to the bank and quickly. But it was after dark and the bank was closed. Why did his evil grin give him the feeling it was already too late?

~

CHARITY SAT in the saloon and stared at the desolate business she loved. What if everything that had been said was true? What if they lost this business? How would Lewis support her and their coming child?

She closed her eyes and did what she'd done during the war when the bombs exploded near her home and she could hear gunfire ricocheting through the city. She prayed and put her trust in God that they would make it through this time.

One more time, she put her faith in him.

The door opened and Quinn and Mr. Huntington walked out the doors.

Lewis slowly approached her, his eyes dark and he ran his hand through his hair. As he stopped in front of her, she stared into his blue eyes and saw the pain reflected from his gaze.

What a terrible day. First, she lost the book with all her tips and now she wondered if she would lose her husband as well.

"Tell me the truth," she said softly. For once, her quick, Irish temper seemed to have dissipated and in its place a searing ache in her chest where she was certain her heart had broken in two. At any moment, she feared her anger would ignite if she lost everything.

"Please believe me when I tell you I planned on telling you everything after Christmas. I never did this to hurt you."

"Tell me now," she whispered, knowing whatever he said would be bad and preparing herself for the worst.

"My real name is Lewis Brown." He paused and stared at her and she wanted to reach out and tell him please just get this over with.

"Last summer, I was mining up in Leadville, Colorado, hiding out from my father who wanted me to become a career military officer. Frankly, I was sick of the war and everything it destroyed. So when my military time was completed, I hid from my father, refusing to continue in the service."

Her husband picked up her hand and held it. "A young kid named Jakob was involved in a shootout in town. Jakob tried to ride away but was injured badly and by the time he reached my cabin, he was close to dying."

A part of her sighed with relief. Though she never believed her husband would murder a man, she worried that somehow he killed Jakob and then took his identity.

Lewis walked away and gazed around the room at the empty bar. "After I got him settled, I rode into town for the doctor, fearing he'd be dead by the time I returned. The doctor did his best to save Jakob, but warned me, it didn't look good."

Those days were dark and filled with a lot of soul searching as he watched the young man slowly die. He tried to nurse the man he became friends with back to health.

"For over a week, I sat by his bed, nursed him and tried to

help him heal. During that time, we talked about our lives, our fathers, and he offered me the saloon. Told me he would never use it and all I had to do was pretend to be Jakob Huntington for a year. Then his father would give the business to him."

Why would he give up being himself just to obtain a saloon? What would compel a man to change his name? Unless he was wanted?

Automatically her hand reached down to her belly. Would her child have a father, or would he go to prison?

Sinking into a chair, his face white, his eyes shadowed. "At the time, I had no intention of ever becoming Jakob. Why would I? On the day that Jakob died, I received a threatening letter from my father. Rejoin the U.S. Army or he would disinherit me and send a patrol looking for me."

Now she understood. Now she knew why he no longer wanted to be Lewis, but why hadn't he stood up to his father?

"If I became Jakob then I could run a bar and be someone other than Lewis Brown. My plan was to purchase the saloon from Mr. Huntington. After all, I'm not his son, so I intended to buy the business when I had the funds."

With a sigh, Lewis put his head in his hands. "After fighting in the war, I was tired of combat and military operations. My father is ashamed of me, yet he wants one of his children in the service, so he can show him off. At the time, I felt like I was handed a solution. Become someone else."

Staring at her, his indigo eyes were dark with hurt. "After I buried Jakob, I took his papers and letters about the saloon and headed to Angel Creek, eager to escape being my father's bastard son."

Taking her hand in his, he stared at her. "A couple of months after I arrived, you came along. At first, I thought after thirty days, I would end our marriage. But you brought a light into my life that was missing. You give me joy and happiness and make me laugh. Our time together has made me happy."

While that made her chest ache a little less, she still had questions he needed to answer.

"Why didn't you face your father and tell him that you didn't want to be in the army any longer?" she asked, wondering why her fearless man would cower in regard to his father.

"Because I'm the bastard son of the Union General Winfred Scott. My father had one night with my mother and I'm the product of their time together.

"The general wanted me in the military, but everyone knew I was his bastard son. And they aren't easy on a man who is the child of an illicit affair. Especially when the man is married to a beautiful high society woman who he shares three lovely children with, including two sons."

From things she heard whispered in Charleston society, she realized how her husband must have suffered at the hands of the men in the military. Now she knew why he didn't want to return and she couldn't blame him. The war had taken so many men and damaged so many others.

"Never will I have a child born out of wedlock. Never will my children suffer the humiliation I've been subjected to. Never."

It didn't bother her that he was a bastard...

The realization slammed into Charity and she swallowed the tears that clogged her throat. A gasp escaped her as her stomach cramped with the knowledge.

"At the time, it became apparent that being Jakob was a great chance to start over. In the end, I'm afraid it backfired on me," Lewis said, gazing at her oddly as she gasped for air.

How did she tell him? How could she let him know his worst fear had been realized?

Suddenly she closed her eyes and bowed her head. "Oh my God, I'm married to a dead man, and I'm expecting your baby. Your illegitimate child."

CHAPTER 13

*A*fter she told him she was expecting, the atmosphere in the house had grown colder than a raging blizzard. Lewis had retreated inside himself so far, she'd given up on trying to reach him. They barely spoke, even in bed, and now she believed he didn't want the baby or her.

Her marriage was over before it barely began and it wasn't even legal. Lewis could walk away and leave her and the baby.

The night had been long and sleepless and now here she stood on Sarah's doorstep.

The sun shone brightly, yet the snow lingered. The need to cry on someone's shoulder had her making her way across frozen slush in the street. Once again, life taught her it could change in an instant and not necessarily for the better.

When she knocked on Sarah's door, she was surprised when Becca answered.

"Hi, Becca," she said. "Where's your mommy?"

"She's inside," she said.

"Can I come in and talk to her?"

"No, she's busy."

Stunned, Charity stood staring at the child. While she

adored this little girl, sometimes she was a little preco-cious. Hopefully having a father would help give the child a little more discipline.

"Well, I need to talk to her right away. It's an emergency."

Oh how she wished Julia and Ruby were here, but they weren't close. And she needed someone to tell her she wasn't a complete fool for falling in love with a man impersonating someone else. How did she cope with being married to a dead man, expecting another man's child?

Sarah came to the door. "Becca, what are you doing?"

"You were with Quinn, so I told Charity you were busy."

"Come in. What's wrong, you look like you haven't slept."

"I haven't," she said, thinking of how she tossed and turned all night long worrying about what to do. How her poor baby was such an innocent caught in a terrible mess of her own doing. If only she'd waited the thirty days, she could have walked away from Lewis.

But could she? She loved this man.

"Becca, I need you to go to your room," Sarah told her.

"Why? So you can talk grown up talk?"

Oh, the little girl was trying her mother.

"That's right. Now go play."

The little girl stomped all the way down the hall, her blonde curls bouncing as she made her feelings known.

Shaking her head, Sarah gazed at Charity. "I'm sorry, but Becca is testing my patience."

Sarah had her hands full trying to get her daughter to adjust to life here in Angel Creek while also dealing with her new husband. Why here at Christmas did it feel like everything was coming apart. They'd been so happy and now she learned it was all a lie.

"Tell me what's going on with you and Lewis. Quinn told me a little last night."

Charity sank down on the couch and put her hands over her

eyes. "Sarah, I'm in so much trouble. I've fallen in love with Lewis, I'm expecting his baby and now I'm married to a dead man named Jakob Huntington."

For the next five minutes, she told Sarah everything Lewis told her, pouring her heart out to her friend. Realizing she was right back where she started, only this time she no longer resided in Charleston. This time the situation looked desperate and this time she'd brought a child into this mayhem.

"We lost the saloon. All the work we did to make the Angel Creek Palace a successful business is gone. Old man Huntington wants us out by the day after Christmas."

Her friend reached out and touched her on the arm. "What are you going to do?"

Last night that question kept her awake all night. After his reaction, she had doubts about everything. What if he left town and vanished?

"All night, I asked myself that question. Lewis said nothing about us getting married. He's never told me he loves me. Last night, he didn't even respond to the fact we're having a baby. And all the money I'd earned and been saving disappeared."

Charity grabbed her handkerchief out of her purse and she wiped her tears. "Once again, I have nothing. Only this time, I'm going to bring a child into the world and I'm penniless."

Squeezing her hand, Sarah said, "You know I'll help you anyway I can."

The tears Charity had held at bay all night and even this morning splashed down her cheeks at her friend's thoughtfulness. "Thank you, but what am I going to do, Sarah? What if Lewis doesn't love me and never marries me? What about the baby?"

All her fears overwhelmed her and the tears cascaded harder down her face. Since last night, she'd kept everything locked up inside, and today she couldn't deal with it anymore.

"Stop, Charity. Remember, I met Lewis and he's a fine man. Give him some time to figure this all out. Have faith things will work out the way they're supposed to."

She leaned on her friend's shoulder. "Thank you. Promise me if something happens and Lewis never marries me, will you raise the baby as your own. This child shouldn't suffer humiliation because his father doesn't want him."

Her friend took a sharp intake of breath. "Of course, I would, but everything is going to work out. After all, we didn't come all this way just to be broken once again. I understand you're scared, but don't give up on Lewis just yet."

ALL NIGHT LEWIS had tossed and turned and blamed himself. If only he had the courage to stand up to his father, this would never have happened. It was all his fault and now another child was stuck in the middle of the situation, along with his beautiful wife.

Only they weren't married and now he feared she would never agree to marry him again. This morning she left before him and he had no clue where she went.

Was she arranging for her return to Charleston? That couldn't happen until spring, and by then, she would be big with his child and...he needed to stop this now.

No, he couldn't leave Montana and return to the military. No, he couldn't meet his father on the battlefield face to face and work this out. But he could send him a letter, telling him his location and he was done.

Taking out the piece of paper, he put the pen to the paper and began the correspondence he should have written months ago instead of assuming another man's name.

Dear General Scott,

This is to inform you I will not be returning to the U.S. Army. If you insist on a court martial, you will need to come to the Montana territory to locate me. After my wound healed was the time to discharge me, but you interfered trying to keep me in the service.

I'm done. No more.

To continue our relationship as father and son, you will need to understand you can never ask me to join the military again. I've married, and soon, we will be having our first child.

As your illegitimate son, I make no claims or expect anything from you. This is not a request for money or anything. It's quite the opposite.

The next move will be on your part. It's your decision if you wish to carry on as father and son, you'll accept I will no longer serve in the military. I'll receive correspondence from you stating that fact. If I don't hear from you, I understand and will not contact you again.

Lewis Brown

Quickly he folded the parchment, sealed it and wrote the address on the envelope. The letter would arrive after the first of the year.

A sense of fulfillment overwhelmed him. No matter the outcome, he'd made his stand. Now all he needed to do was find a way to support his wife and baby. And pray the town forgave him for impersonating another man.

STEPPING INSIDE THE BANK, Lewis glanced at the teller who saw him come strolling in. "Mr. Jones, I need to pull some money out of the saloon's account."

The bank man sighed and shook his head. "I'm sorry, Lewis. That Huntington fellow closed the account yesterday. Cleaned it out. Thought it odd, but his name was listed on the paperwork and nothing I could do to stop him."

For a moment, Lewis stood there, reeling. Everything he worked for in the last six months, taken. All the hard work of making the saloon a success. All the money he saved hoping to buy out the owner. But now everything was legally stolen because of his stupidity.

And his wife -- no Jakob's wife, expecting his baby and he promised himself he would never have an illegitimate child. How had he gotten himself into such a mess and how could he fix it?

The money he had on him was all he had. Old man Huntington gave them until the day after Christmas to get out of the apartment.

"Thanks, Mr. Jones. It was a pleasure doing business with you."

"Heard he shut down the saloon last night? Is it true?"

The news must be all over town. Lewis Brown was a fool for trying to become more than the bastard son of a general.

"Yes, he did. I should never have impersonated his son, though he told me too."

The banker nodded. "You did a great job, you and your wife, Charity. Maybe you should open a new saloon."

"All the money I had was in that account and now it's gone."

The man nodded. "Are you going to stay in town?"

Lewis thought of his options and realized he didn't want to leave Angel Creek. The little town felt like home and he wanted to stay here, but that would depend on Charity.

All he wanted was to be with her until death did they part. Then again, they weren't legally married and now that she knew he was a bastard, she may not want to marry him. And he couldn't blame her since he failed her as a husband.

"Don't know what the future holds for us."

Lewis kept saying *us* because Charity was his wife, not Jakob's, but his. Maybe their marriage wasn't legal, but in his heart, she belonged to him. Together they said their vows.

Last night's events shocked him so badly, he probably hadn't expressed his feelings very well. After everything, he needed time to make sense of what happened.

No matter what, if she would accept him, he wanted to marry her again. He wanted his son or daughter not to be born out of wedlock. He wanted to spend his days with Charity making him laugh and the two of them working and walking together on this journey of life.

He loved Charity and couldn't wait to express to her his love. She needed to understand how much he needed her. How much he loved her. How he wanted to remarry her as soon as possible.

CHAPTER 14

*C*harity walked into the apartment, her long full skirts swishing and found Lewis pacing the floor. When she came in the door, he stopped walking and stared at her, his blue eyes sparkling with what appeared to be tears. "Thank God, there you are. I was so worried."

"Why?" she asked, her frustration with him seeping into her voice. "I went to talk to Sarah."

"Oh, I feared you had given up on me," he said.

How did she respond? Part of her said pack her bags and leave and the other part said, no, wait and let him tell her his intentions.

"How could I leave," she said. "We're pretty much snowed in and I have no money."

"But you thought about it," he said, gazing at her, his expression filled with hurt. Could he care?

"Can you blame me? I'm frightened. I'm pregnant and I'm not married. And even if we were married, I'm not certain who you are anymore. I'm not certain about the man I've fallen in love with."

In two steps, Lewis was by her side. He handed her a small

box. "Open it. I bought this almost a week ago before our lives fell apart."

Could this be what she hoped it was?

Stunned, she stared at the small gift. With trembling fingers, she tore the wrapping paper and opened the box. Inside was a gold band. A wedding ring.

"Look on the inside," he said.

"My Irish Love," she said, her heart bursting with love as she wept.

Lewis loved her and that overcame everything that happened in the last twenty-four hours. Together they would find a way.

"I love you, Charity. You exploded into my life and took my heart prisoner. You make me laugh, we have fun, you're the part of me that is missing. If you'll have me, I want to spend the rest of my life with you."

Reaching out, she cupped his cheek.

He continued. "Since the night we slept together, it's laid heavy on my mind about how I hadn't told you the truth about who I was, but I never dreamed we were not legally married. As the bastard son of a Union general, I always said I would never have children out of wedlock. Yet here because of my own stupidity, we aren't considered married and we're expecting a baby, that I want so very much."

Her heart gave her a kick in the chest when he got down on one knee and stared up into her face. Charity knew her life would never be the same. "Will you please marry me and make me a legal husband and a proud father? Only you will make me the happiest man in the territory."

Tears trickled out of Charity's eyes as she gazed at this man who made some terrible mistakes, but then again, hadn't they both. She had vandalized her own home in retaliation and he'd stood by her.

Now it was her turn to stand by Lewis as his loving wife and the mother of his children. More than anything, she would stand beside him because she loved him with all her heart.

"Yes, Lewis, I'll marry you. I love you so much," she said, pulling him to his feet. They stood there holding one another and she realized they almost lost each other before they had a chance to begin. "Promise me you'll never keep anything from me ever again."

"Cross my heart, I promise."

Stepping out of his arms, she opened a drawer and pulled out a wrapped gift for him. "Almost a week ago, I purchased this for you. We had the same plans. On Christmas Day, I was going to tell you I loved you and that I'm with child. But life had other surprises for us."

Though it felt anticlimactic, she gave him the small box and he smiled. "Promise me you won't ever leave me."

"Never," she said. "In sickness and in health, until death do we part."

Lewis ripped the package open and lifted the lid of the box. A smile crossed his face as he removed the gold band from the box and slipped it on his finger. Staring at her, his eyes brimmed with moisture. "What if we married tonight, Christmas Eve, at the church? Do you think the reverend would marry us?"

"That sounds like a wonderful plan," she said, laughing.

"I think so too," he said, taking her into his arms and kissing her like he would never let her go. Charity sighed as his lips moved over hers.

Sarah was right. Her man just needed some time to work things out.

LATER THAT EVENING, as Charity and Lewis walked to the Christmas Eve gathering at the church, she held a small sack with the donations from the saloon party for the McGregor family. The thought had crossed her mind more than once that it would be so easy to take the money since they were basically penniless, but that wouldn't be right.

People had donated to help the family reach San Francisco and she was determined they would receive the money tonight. This had been part of her charity work and she would uphold her honor.

"Are you ready to marry me again," Lewis asked as they walked up the steps to the church.

She grinned at the man she planned on walking through life with. "Tell me, Mr. Brown, what do you want in a wife?"

Would Lewis remember the words they said to each other when they first met in this very same building?

Halting, he pulled her in his arms and smiled at her. "You, darlin'. You."

"Always and forever," she said, giving him a quick kiss.

They were laughing when he opened the door and saw the townspeople gathered, waiting for them. "Surprise."

In shock, she stared at the people they had gotten to know in the small town.

"What?" Lewis asked, appearing stunned. "It's a Christmas party."

"And a wedding," the reverend said, smiling. "That is if you two want to marry, well, remarry." There was no question about it. The minister's grin said he knew the answer.

Joe stepped up. "The two of you are a big part of our community. Since you joined our little town, the saloon has grown and become a place where men can gather. Mrs. Charity, you have helped so many in our town. So tonight, we're honored to repay your kindness."

The man set an empty basket next to the tables of prepared food. "All the money collected goes to the two of you. Our prayer is that enough will be donated to help you purchase or start a new saloon."

Charity threw her hands over her face as tears rolled down her cheeks and then turned to Lewis who squeezed her tightly. "We're going to be all right."

"We didn't expect this," Lewis said, his throat groggy sounding like it was full of tears.

"Sometimes we all need a little help," Isaac said as he came from the shadows and dumped the contents of the book into the basket, making the first donation. "After I found the money, I tried to leave town, but I couldn't. Because you two have taken care of me."

Charity reached out and hugged him. She hoped he would always be a part of their lives. "When I couldn't find you, it gave me such a fright."

"I'm sorry. Since the robbery when my parents died, I've wanted to return home. But I quickly realized Angel Creek, here with you and Lewis, is my new home."

Lewis grasped them both in a hug. "Isaac, we're so proud of the man you're becoming. Stay with us."

Then she watched as the men she'd befriended and listened to each night, one by one, walked up and dropped money in the container.

Even her friends, Sarah, Ruby, Julie, and Anna donated money to help them.

She gazed at the man she loved and knew they had found a place to call home. Angel Creek, Montana, would be where they would raise their children and spend the rest of their days together.

"I love you so much, Lewis," she said.

Holding her, he whispered in her ear, "This is all because of you, my Irish love. Now, marry me, before one of these fine gentlemen tries to steal you away from me."

"I'm always yours," she said and took him by the hand.

～

THE STORY AT ITS END, Charity rocked in her old chair and glanced at the children in the room. Some sat intently listening while the younger kids had fallen asleep. The older ones knew she'd left out some of the juicer details, but still they sat enthralled at the life she and Lewis led.

"Great-grandmother, how much money did they collect for you and Grandpa?" The youngest Brown family member asked.

It was a figure she never divulged to anyone. Truly a Christmas miracle from the small town. They received enough that they purchased the Angel Creek Palace from old man Huntington and bought a small house. In the end, they continued their work of helping others in the community. Even renaming the saloon to Jakob's Place.

Because, after all, if that young man had not given Lewis the opportunity, they would never have met.

Isaac became their son and his grandchildren sat amongst the kids in the room.

The sheriff and the doctor collaborated Lewis's story of the gunfight and Jakob's death. The doctor even praised Lewis for trying to save the young man.

Months went by and Lewis never heard from his father. Years later, they learned of his death, but he never spoke to the general again.

"What happened to Julia and Matthew? They're my great-grandparents," a little boy sitting on the floor asked.

"Julia," Charity called and her friend shuffled into the family room. The years had aged her, but at this time in life, they all felt blessed to be upright and not six feet under.

"Your great-grandson wants to know your story," she said.

She grinned. "Well..."

～

Julia's story continues in book 2 by Lily Graison

Julia Hamel always dreamed of a Christmas wedding and hers would be a dream come true if she wasn't marrying a man she'd never met. Traveling across the country as a mail-order bride took a leap of faith, and she's determined to make the best of her new life despite that fact her husband seems to be hiding something. But nothing she does seems to please him and Matthew's distant despite her best intentions. When she meets a mischievous old man and takes his advice on how to make her husband happy, his ideas backfire in the worst possible ways and as Christmas draws closer, Julia begins to think leaving home may have been the worst mistake of her life.

Matthew Bailey never wanted a wife—until he saw Julia. He married her without much thought and hoped her presence would be enough to finally distract him from the fact it was the one time of year he wished he could forget. Painful memories keep him distracted and when the girl who mistook his kindness for a wedding proposal stirs up trouble, Matthew has to decide what he really wants. If its Julia, then he has to bare his soul and confront his past but dredging up those old memories is still painful. Can the love of a woman he knows nothing about be enough to make him want to live again? And will Julia stay once she's seen the worst in him?

PLEASE LEAVE A REVIEW

Did you enjoy the book? Reviews help authors. I would appreciate you posting a review. Click here to leave a review.

Follow Sylvia McDaniel on Facebook.

Sign up for my New Book Alert and receive a complimentary book.

Find Them Only At Amazon

Charleston isn't what it used to be. The war has left it in ruins and the chance of a suitable marriage almost obsolete. Five friends take a daring leap and head west for a new life and possible love match as Mail-Order brides. After finding their happily ever afters, they invite more of their friends to join them, and soon, Angel Creek, Montana is invaded by Southern Belles all looking for love and the town will never be the same.

CHRISTMAS 2018 BOOKS
Book 1: Charity — Sylvia McDaniel
Book 2: Julia — Lily Graison
Book 3: Ruby — Hildie McQueen
Book 4: Sarah — Peggy McKenzie
Book 5: Anna — Everly West

CHRISTMAS 2019 BOOKS
Book 6: Caroline — Lily Graison
Book 7: Melody — Caroline Clemmons
Book 8: Emma — Peggy McKenzie
Book 9: Viola — Cyndi Raye
Book 10: Ginger — Sylvia McDaniel

CHRISTMAS 2020 BOOKS
Book 11: Abigail — Peggy McKenzie
Book 12: Pearl — Hildie McQueen
Book 13: Rebecca — Lily Graison
Book 14: Charlotte — Kari Trumbo

Book 15: Minnie — Sylvia McDaniel
Book 16: Adele — Cynthia Woolf
Book 17: Victoria — Maxine Douglas
Book 18: Meg — Caroline Clemmons

CHRISTMAS 2021 BOOKS
Book 19: Glenda — Hildie McQueen
Book 20: Temperance — Lily Graison
Book 21: Hannah — Peggy McKenzie
Book 22: Amy — Caroline Clemmons
Book 23: Cora — Sylvia McDaniel

Find Them All At Amazon.Com

Look for the new series Mistletoe Falls Christmas Brides

Gossip spread through the orphanage faster than fire in a hay barn. One by one, all the girls, now educated young ladies, were leaving and in typical Madam Wigg fashion: orderly alphabetical sequence by first name. Unfortunately, she'd reached the Ns and Quinlan's dormitory room could only be next.

"Can you hear her? Is Madam Wigg coming this way or not?"

Quinlan Clark had lived in fear for the last few months dreading this day, doubting there was any way to avoid the change heading at her like a steam engine. Madam Wigg was slowly dismantling her school, sending the orphans she had raised to teach into the world to spread education to children in need.

Rumors swirled about the school that Madam Wigg was dying, but Quinlan wasn't so certain. The woman was strong and healthy though a little doddering in her old age. Quinlan leaned closer to the door, a hand cupped around her ear, hoping the bell tolled for someone other than the girls she shared a room with.

"Shh. It's hard to hear." Phebe stood in front of Quinlan with one side of her face pressed against the closed entrance. "I'm sure it's her, and she's definitely coming this way."

Madam Wigg had a thing for order and she placed them in rooms A to Z and some of the orphans she'd even named in alphabet order. It was an easy way to know where each girl was located. When Quinlan arrived at the age of seven, she was already named, but she would never forget when Madam Wigg smiled and said, *I was needing a girl with a Q name.* And so began a nice, stable, quiet life minus screaming. And she didn't want the pleasant experience to change.

"Do you think it's our turn to be told about her illness and this whole mail-order bride thing?" Olivia's slender frame was crowded next to Quinlan. A worried look had crept into her brown eyes.

Nellie clasped her hands together as her lips began to tremble. "I hope not. I don't like the idea at all. It's... well, it's..."

The four had shared this room since they were children, growing up together, becoming more like sisters than roommates in the orphanage. Now at twenty-five, Quinlan hoped they were too old to marry. Marriage meant...she shuddered as the memories from her childhood flooded her.

Years ago, she'd come to the realization that she was fortunate to have been taken to the Wigg School and Foundling Home. And the thought of picking someone from a newspaper ad for a husband sent fear slithering along her spine like a snake, causing her to shake.

What if this unknown man was like her father?

Footsteps halted at their door.

Phebe stepped back, grabbed Olivia's hand and gave Quinlan a gentle shove, shooing the other three friends. "We need to sit on our beds. I think Madam Wigg is right outside."

A sharp, double rap against wood confirmed Phebe's words as the friends ran to their beds. Everyone but Phebe sat just as the door swung open and their mentor swept into the room like a queen, her hands holding a bundle of papers behind her back. What was in her fingers?

Terror seized Quinlan's chest. The rumors were true. They were being sent into the world she had avoided since she was a child. This was her safe haven, her place of peace, and Madam Wigg would soon force her to leave.

Phebe stood alone in the middle of the room, facing their mentor.

"I'm surprised to catch you eavesdropping, Phebe. It doesn't suit you at all."

Phebe tensed, her cheeks blushing as she gazed at Madam Wigg like she was confronting a student.

"I apologize, Madam, but it does have its uses at times."

Years ago, the girls had learned it was better to admit their faults to Madam Wigg when they misbehaved. The punishment was far less and she even kind of admired the fact you were honest about your wrong doings. It kept Quinlan from the study hall having to write she would never repeat her offense a thousand times more than once.

The older woman chuckled. "Yes, it does." She looked at the other three and nodded. "I've come to talk to all of you about a serious matter."

Quinlan feared she was going to be ill, right here in front of her mentor. Because the very thought of giving up her safe home left her terrified.

"You aren't really sick, are you?" Olivia blurted, then clamped her lips together when Madam Wigg gave an exasperated sigh.

Oh boy, Olivia was never one for glossing things over. She went straight for the jugular and wanted the truth of the matter. No one tried to fool her black-as-ink haired friend, because she would put them in their place in a heartbeat.

"I know you girls talk among yourselves, so I'm sure you've already heard about my illness. Which means there's no need to dwell on that." She pointed at Phebe and Quinlan. "Now, the two of you join Nellie and Olivia and have a seat. Then I'll explain what we're going to do about this little problem."

Why couldn't Madam Wigg at least confirm or deny or even tell them what was wrong with her? Didn't she know they all worried about her and would never leave her alone during this terrible time. Then again, the woman sometimes pushed them away when she felt they needed to be stronger and she was all about her charges being capable women.

"It isn't a little problem, Madam," Phebe interrupted softly. She sank down on the bed next to Nellie and frowned at her mentor. "If you're sick, we need to stay and take care of you, not go flitting off to secure new positions as if you didn't mean anything to us."

Nellie took one of Phebe's hands in her own and held on tightly. "That's right." A sheen of moisture glistened in her friend's eyes as she stared back at Madam Wigg. "We should be here to take care of you.

Why didn't the girls understand, Quinlan wondered. If Madam Wigg was truly sick and dying, she would never want her girls to see her weak and debilitated. The woman had a rigid, puritanical, stoical air about her that would never submit to letting others see her as being weak. Even in sickness. Didn't they remember when she had pneumonia the year before and forbade anyone but Cook and the doctor from entering her room?

The women chimed in agreement until the older woman held up a hand, her palm facing outward like a warning sign.

"I appreciate your concern. I really do. But I am still head of this school, and I say it's time you all stopped worrying about me and made your own way in this world." She set a stack of papers tied with a string on top of the lone table in the cozy-sized room. "*The Bride's Bulletin* is filled with advertisements of men looking for wives. Any one of them can give you a home and help you get started teaching. If you pick wisely."

That was the problem. Quinlan knew nothing about men and wouldn't know how to choose a man if her life depended on it and obviously, right now, it did. The only man she'd known had been ripped out of her life for good reasons. Since then, she'd avoided men.

"You girls haven't had a chance to do much choosing in your lives," Madam Wigg's voice softened as she looked at each of them, her eyes growing warm. "You had no choice in coming here, or in the work you were given to do. The only choice you've all made for yourselves was to stay and learn to be teachers.

"Now it's time for you to make another choice. This time to select a husband, so you can give something back to other children who need a teacher. Every child deserves to be educated and have an opportunity to do well when they grow up."

Quinlan completely agreed that every child deserved an education, even the poor, the downtrodden, the children of criminals. Everyone. But how did one go about selecting a husband when you didn't know what were good qualities in a man? How did you find someone who agreed with your desire to educate children?

Madam pointed at the papers. "Look those prospects over carefully, but don't select one with a mark by his notice. He's already been spoken for by one of the other girls. And once you've settled on one, don't forget to put your mark down too. I don't want to hear about any squabbles going on over some poor man no one has even met."

What could she do? Where would she go? Gingerly she picked up the newspaper and started to thumb through the pages, shocked by the number of lonely men in the world searching for a wife.

Madam Wigg turned and made her way back to the door where she paused. "Phebe?"

"Yes, ma'am."

"You look the notices over and then come to my sitting room. I need to speak with you privately."

Quinlan scanned the many ads. She had one chance to get this right or find herself in the same situation as her mother. Remembering her history lessons, whoever she chose, he had to be from Texas.

Without another word, the older woman sailed out the door, leaving an anxious group of women.

Quinlan laughed out loud as she read the ridiculous requests of some of the men. "Phebe, come over here. You have to read these."

The papers were open on the table and all three of the other women were crowded around them, pointing at the notices covering every page.

"Oh heavens." Olivia blinked as she leaned closer, squinting at the small print. "This gentleman specifically mentions that he's looking for a woman with a strong back and good constitution."

This was why Quinlan didn't want a man. Her insides tightened at the memory of her father and the work he required of her mother. Why couldn't she skip the marriage part and just have her own children? What did she need with a man? "Sounds like he's mixed up a wife with a plow horse."

Nellie clasped her hands together and gave Phebe an uncertain look. "I don't know about this. However are we supposed to choose?"

Great question. How could she discern the abusers from the good men? And what if all men, even the good ones, could become a wife beater? A shiver rattled her bones.

Olivia shrugged at Nellie before putting an arm around Phebe's shoulders and drawing her next to the table. "Well,

QUINLAN'S QUEST

Phebe's only going to be looking for a gentleman from California." She gave her friend a questioning glance. "Unless you've changed your mind about that promise to your mama?"

Drawing in a deep breath, she straightened her spine and smiled at the women before she bent over the paper and ran a finger down the first page.

"Now. Let's see what we have here."

Quinlan sighed. There was no getting out of this. The time had come to pick her future or maybe her death.

Available at Your Favorite Retailer

157

Also By Sylvia McDaniel
Western Historicals
A Hero's Heart
Second Chance Cowboy
Ethan

American Brides
**Katie: Bride of Virginia

Angel Creek Christmas Brides
**Charity
**Ginger
**Minnie
**Cora

Bad Girls of the West
Scandalous Sadie
Ravenous Rose
Tempting Tessa
Nellie's Redemption

The Burnett Brides Series
The Rancher Takes A Bride
The Outlaw Takes A Bride
The Marshal Takes A Bride
The Christmas Bride
Boxed Set

Lipstick and Lead Series
Desperate
Deadly
Dangerous

Daring
**Determined
Deceived
Defiant
Devious
Lipstick and Lead Box Set Books 1-4
Lipstick and Lead Box Set Books 5-9
Lipstick and Lead Box Set Books 1-9
**Quinlan's Quest

Mail Order Bride Tales
**A Brother's Betrayal
**Pearl
**Ace's Bride

Scandalous Suffragettes of the West
**Abigail
Bella
Mistletoe Scandal

Southern Historical Romance
A Scarlet Bride
**Belle

The Cuvier Women
Wronged
Betrayed
Beguiled
Boxed Set

The Debutante's of Durango
The Debutante's Scandal
The Debutante's Gamble
The Debutante's Revenge

The Debutante's Santa

** Denotes a sweet book.

Want to learn about my new releases before anyone else?
Sign up for my New Book Alert at www.SylviaMcDaniel.com
and receive a complimentary book.

USA Today Best-selling author, Sylvia McDaniel obviously has too much time on her hands. With over eighty western historical and contemporary romance novels, she spends most days torturing her characters. Bad boys deserve punishment and even good girls get into trouble. Always looking for the next plot twist, she's known for her sweet, funny, family-oriented romances.

Married to her best friend for over twenty-five years, they recently moved to the state of Colorado where they like to hike, and enjoy the beauty of the forest behind their home with their spoiled dachshund Zeus and puppy Bailey. (He has his own column in her newsletter.)

Their grown son, still lives in Texas. An avid football watcher, she loves the Broncos and the Cowboys, especially when they're winning.

www.SylviaMcDaniel.com
Sylvia@SylviaMcDaniel.com
The End!

www.ingramcontent.com/pod-product-compliance
Lightning Source LLC
Chambersburg PA
CBHW072237190626
46809CB00018B/2714